THE GIRLS'
BOOK
of
FLOWER
FAIRIES
T.M

THE PINK FAIRIES

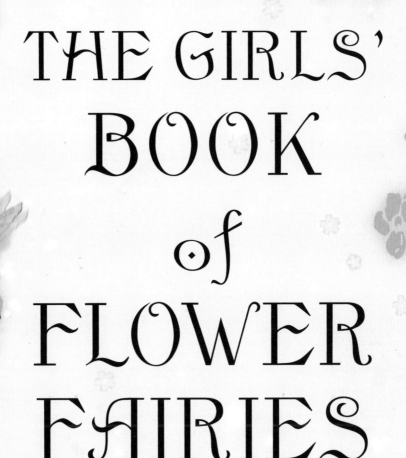

THE GIRLS'
BOOK
of
FLOWER
FAIRIES

_{T.M}

FREDERICK WARNE

FREDERICK WARNE

Published by the Penguin Group
Penguin Books Ltd, 80 Strand, London WC2R 0RL, England
Penguin Young Readers Group, 1745 Broadway, New York, New York 10019, USA
Penguin Group (Canada), 90 Eglinton Avenue East, Suite 700, Toronto, Ontario, Canada M4P 2Y3
Penguin Ireland, 25 St Stephen's Green, Dublin 2, Ireland
Penguin Books Australia Ltd, 707 Collins Street, Melbourne, Victoria 3008, Australia
Penguin Books India (P) Ltd, 11 Community Centre, Panchsheel Park, New Delhi 110 017, India
Penguin Group (NZ), 67 Apollo Drive, Rosedale, North Shore 0632, New Zealand
Penguin Books (South Africa) (Pty) Ltd, Block D, Rosebank Office Park,
181 Jan Smuts Avenue, Parktown North, Gauteng 2193, South Africa

Penguin Books Ltd, Registered Offices: 80 Strand, London WC2R 0RL, England

Web site at: www.flowerfairies.com

First published by Frederick Warne 2008
Copyright © Frederick Warne & Co., 2008
New reproductions of Cicely Mary Barker's illustrations copyright © The Estate of Cicely Mary Barker, 1990
Original illustrations copyright © The Estate of Cicely Mary Barker, 1923, 1925, 1926, 1934,
1940, 1944, 1948

ISBN: 978 0 7232 6273 2

Printed in China

CONTENTS

What Is a Flower Fairy?

Have you ever seen—or thought you saw—a fairy? Perhaps you caught sight of a tiny wing glittering in the sunlight? Maybe you heard the sound of tinkling laughter coming from the garden? If so, you may have been lucky enough to glimpse a magical Flower Fairy.

Flower Fairies are lovely little creatures, about 5 to 7 inches tall, who live among flowers, plants, and trees. They have sweet faces, soft hair, and beautiful fluttering wings. Some fairies are girls, others are boys.

Each Flower Fairy lives and sleeps in his or her own special plant. They wear outfits made from its leaves and flowers, so it is easy for them to hide. Fairies are shy little creatures and will disappear very quickly if they are scared.

Flower Fairy Characteristics

Flower Fairies are kind, sweet, and helpful, although some of them can be a little mischievous at times! And while every fairy has a unique personality, all fairies have certain things in common. They love music and dancing and will always find a reason to get together for a chat or to throw a party. Tea parties are especially popular with fairies, because they enjoy preparing —and eating—delicious fairy food and drink.

Flower Fairies are also known as nature sprites, and the environment is very important to them. They do all they can to look after the plants and flowers that grow around them, and they live happily alongside the wild creatures that make their homes nearby. In fact, Flower Fairies make friends with most animals and insects, and they help one another out as much as possible—fairies will even hitch lifts with grasshoppers and fly alongside birds so that they are less likely to be spotted.

Flower Fairies are happy little creatures. They sometimes worry about the weather or about humans picking their plants or dropping rubbish nearby. But generally they are calm and contented.

FINDING A FLOWER FAIRY

Flower Fairies can be found resting against the stems of flowers, balancing on leaves, swinging from the branches of trees—in fact, just about anywhere that plants grow. However, fairies are wary of humans, whom they find very big and loud, so they will always try and hide themselves. Fairies have extra-sensitive ears, so if they hear someone approaching they will quickly flutter into a flower or other handy hiding place and curl up tightly. If you are looking for a fairy, you will have to be very patient and determined, as they are not easy to find.

But remember, the more you know about fairies, the more likely it is that you will see one. This book tells you everything you need to know about the world of the Flower Fairies so that you will know exactly what to look for. Good luck!

Flower
Fairy
Appearances

Boy fairies have pointed ears.

Some fairies wear hats made from flowers or nut shells.

Flower Fairies are never found very far from their flower or tree.

Every fairy wears a unique outfit made from the petals and leaves of his or her special plant.

Fairies' delicate wings are often mistaken for a butterfly's.

Fairies occasionally wear shoes, but most go barefoot.

WHERE?

Where are the fairies?
    Where can we find them?
We've seen the fairy-rings
    They leave behind them!

Is it a secret
    No one is telling?
Why, in your garden
    Surely they're dwelling!

No need for journeying,
    Seeking afar;
Where there are flowers
    There fairies are!

FAIRY HOMES

FLOWER FAIRY HOMES are all around you, but they are cleverly hidden. A human would not recognize a Flower Fairy home. We would simply see a few blades of grass, a pile of twigs and leaves, or a flower bed bursting with glorious blooms!

Of all the Flower Fairies, garden fairies are the most sociable. Many of them live in parks or town gardens, so they are used to traffic noise and human voices. Garden fairies enjoy company. They are confident, friendly, and talkative!

Tulip is always welcome in the garden.

Wallflower loves to sit high up on the wall.

Delicate and pretty, wild Flower Fairies live peacefully alongside country lanes and footpaths. They play together, and sometimes you can hear them calling to each other. Their voices sound just like birdsong and are carried along on the breeze.

The windswept fields and meadows are home to nomadic grass fairies. They have no particular home, and at night they just crawl under a leaf to sleep.

Rush-Grass and Cotton-Grass guide travelers across the moors.

Wild Cherry Blossom sits among her clouds of white blooms.

Treetop fairies are the most daring and athletic of all Flower Fairies. The blossom fairies have no fear of heights. They are happiest swinging from branch to branch high up in their trees. They are the fairy acrobats!

Lilac blossoms have the sweetest scent of all.

Watery fairies play near their homes on the banks of rivers and streams. Sometimes you can hear their silvery voices, which sound a bit like running water.

Willow dips her toes in the cool water.

Naughty Horse Chestnut lives high in the trees.

Beechnut is the naughtiest of all.

The youngest nut fairies are the naughtiest, playing noisy games of chase in their branches. If you are walking under a beech tree on a blustery day, it is not the wind that sends beechnuts raining down on to your head!

Alder loves to play by the river.

Look up, look up, at any tree!
There is so much for eyes to see:
And, if you're quick enough, maybe
A laughing fairy in the tree!

Iris plays at the water's edge.

Living in the Garden

Did you know there could be hundreds of Flower Fairies living in your garden? There are many different places where fairies might be hiding. Hanging baskets, potted plants, and rock gardens are all good spots for cozy fairy homes. But the place where most garden fairies live is in the flower bed, close to their favorite flowers.

Against this colorful background, Flower Fairies live in sociable groups, talking, working, and playing throughout the day.

The biggest chatterbox is the CANDYTUFT Fairy, who loves talking with her fairy friends. The youngest Flower Fairies adore her because she tells them stories at bedtime—and she always has sticky sweets to give them!

The TULIP Fairy has come from far away, from the land of Persia. She is very wise and has seen a great many things, so the fairies always come to her for advice. She also tells wonderful stories about faraway lands.

A tub

Small stones

Potting soil

Three or four
flowering plants

Garden spade

Sand

RED CLOVER'S FLOWER GARDEN

Red Clover lives right at the end of the garden. She'd like to show you how to make a little Flower Fairy haven of your very own.

1. Find a suitable container for your fairy garden, such as an old tub. Ask an adult before you use it!

2. Place stones at the bottom of the container. Fill the container almost to the top with potting soil.

3. Hold the stems of a plant near the soil and gently slide it out of its pot.

4. Dig a hole in the soil, near the edge. Put the plant in and press the soil down.

5. Add more plants and flowers around the outside of your container. Give them all a drink of water.

6. If you can find some, cover the soil with moss. You could also add a path of sand or small stones.

Plants with tiny flowers will look best. Try:
forget-me-nots
candytuft
violets
lobelia.

You will need:

Cardboard

Ruler

Yellow crepe paper

Pencil

Scissors

Glue

Darning needle
(ask an adult for help in using this)

Embroidery thread

Two twigs

DECORATING YOUR FAIRY GARDEN

White Bryony lives in the hedge, close to Red Clover.
Here she shows you how to decorate your flower garden.

PAPER LANTERNS

1. Draw a triangle on a piece of cardboard, 1 inch wide at its base and 20 inches long.

2. Cut out the card. Draw around it six times on crepe paper. Cut out each shape.

3. Roll each triangle tightly around a pencil, starting at the wide end.

 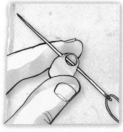 

4. Glue down the pointed end of the paper. Slide off the pencil.

5. Thread a darning needle with embroidery thread. Push needle through each lantern.

6. Tie the ends of the thread around two twigs, and string up your lanterns.

MORE FAIRY IDEAS!

Use glass beads to decorate your path.

Add a tiny fairy-sized tea set!

Make painted tables and chairs from salt dough. (See page 139 for recipe)

Use a mirror for a magical fairy pool!

Make a clothesline and hang fairy laundry.

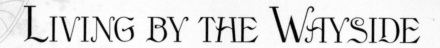
Living by the Wayside

Wild fairies of all kinds can be found among the tall grasses, flowers, and dense hedgerows of the countryside. Whenever you walk down a country path or through a field, there is sure to be a fairy nearby, listening intently until the sound of your footsteps disappears.

Hedgerows provide good homes for large communities of fairies who hide among the thick, deep leaves and brambles. Now and again a fairy will make an appearance, perhaps to chat to a grass fairy or to fly within a passing cloud of butterflies to visit a fairy friend. If a fairy is traveling a long way, she might drop a trail of petals or nuts to help her find the way back home.

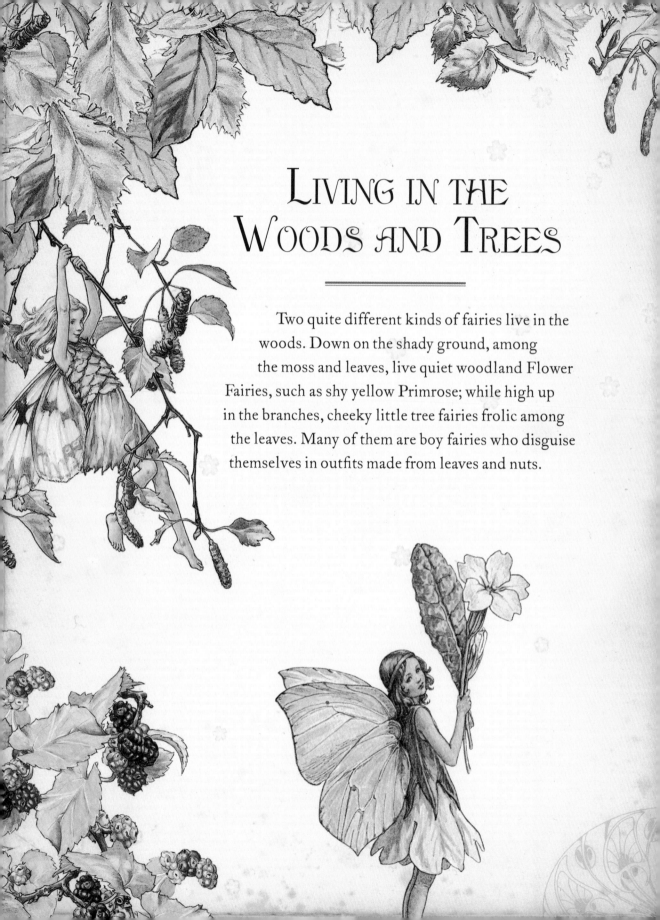

Living in the Woods and Trees

Two quite different kinds of fairies live in the
woods. Down on the shady ground, among
the moss and leaves, live quiet woodland Flower
Fairies, such as shy yellow Primrose; while high up
in the branches, cheeky little tree fairies frolic among
the leaves. Many of them are boy fairies who disguise
themselves in outfits made from leaves and nuts.

Though very different in personality, both ground and tree fairies get on well. The tree fairies will often leap down from the branches to visit their friends below, but if they hear someone coming they will quickly flutter back to the safety of their treetop homes.

Living near Water and Marshland

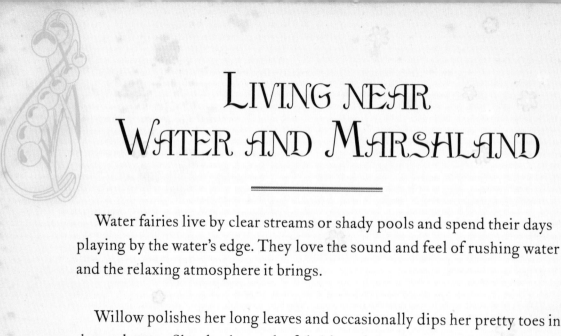

Water fairies live by clear streams or shady pools and spend their days playing by the water's edge. They love the sound and feel of rushing water and the relaxing atmosphere it brings.

Willow polishes her long leaves and occasionally dips her pretty toes into the cool water. She also has a playful side and may be spotted swinging across the stream on one of her long, drooping branches.

Peaceful White Bindweed kneels by the water's edge whispering messages into her beautiful flower. Like all Flower Fairies she takes great care of her special plant.

By the peaceful stream or the shady pool
I dip my leaves in the water cool.

Over the water I lean all day,
Where the sticklebacks and the minnows play.

I dance, I dance, when the breezes blow,
And dip my toes in the stream below.

Spring Magic

The World is very old;
    But year by year
It groweth new again
    When buds appear.
The World is very old,
    And sometimes sad;
But when the daisies come
    The World is glad.
The World is very old;
    But every Spring
It groweth young again,
    And fairies sing.

Fairies
and
the
Seasons

EACH SEASON sees a new group of fairies appearing as their plants come alive and bloom. Some fairies have plants or flowers that bloom in more than one season, but these fairies will still have their favorite time of the year!

SPRING

Spring's arrival marks the beginning of new life. The trees come into bud, tiny new shoots poke their way through the soil, and hundreds of beautiful flowers burst into color. While humans enjoy the sight of all this blossoming, new fairies come out of their winter hibernation into the warmth of the spring sun.

The ALMOND BLOSSOM Fairy is first to appear, gleefully leading the other fairies in a dance to welcome the spring.

There is no surer sign of spring than the sight of a group of yellow daffodils. When the DAFFODIL Fairy makes her appearance she looks beautiful in a dress made from her flower's characteristic "trumpet."

The BLUEBELL Fairy rings his bells to celebrate the new season. The sound can be heard throughout the woods.

My hundred thousand bells of blue,
The splendor of the Spring,
They carpet all the woods anew
With royalty of sapphire hue.

SUMMER

Summer fairies love nothing more than basking upon their petals, feeling the sun's warm rays. The long, hot days provide the perfect opportunity to relax, and summer fairies are probably the most leisurely of all the fairies. It is also the time for outdoor parties and picnics in the Flower Fairy Garden.

The ROSE Fairy tiptoes about her plant, picking off the old petals from her flowers. She chooses the softest petals to dress in and is never hurt by her own thorns. Rose gives gifts of perfumed rose water to the other fairies in the garden.

Carrying a pile of his precious red berries, STRAWBERRY is on his way to a fairy picnic. He is generous with his delicious fruit and very popular with his many fairy friends!

MARIGOLD is usually found in the sunniest spot. She loves to soak up the sunshine, and her vivid color reflects the sun's golden rays.

Great Sun above me in the sky,
So golden, glorious, and high,
My petals, see, are golden too;
They shine, but cannot shine like you.

Autumn

With the onset of autumn comes a dramatic change. As leaves fall from the trees, the woods are colored golden brown. The bright flowers of summer are replaced by shiny brown nuts and dark berries. Now the autumn fairies emerge into the golden light, unfurling their wings in the cool damp air.

The ACORN Fairy lives high up in the branches of the oak tree. His hat is a cup made from one of his precious acorns.

When dusk falls, MICHAELMAS DAISY sprinkles fairy dust into the yellow middles of his flowers. The gleaming blossoms become lanterns lighting up tiny fairy paths around the garden.

The mischievous HORSE CHESTNUT Fairy shakes his spiky-skinned fruits down from the branches. He loves to watch the children play conkers with them!

During showers NASTURTIUM lends his flat leaves to other fairies to use as umbrellas. By the time the winter snow blows in, Nasturtium is sleeping and nowhere to be found.

Nasturtium the jolly,
O ho, O ho!
He holds up his brolly
Just so, just so!

WINTER

The golden days of autumn soon turn into the chill of winter. But there is always something sparkling in the garden. Snowdrops and crocuses bravely push their fragile stems through the frozen ground, while ice crystals glisten on the wings of winter fairies as they tend their plants in the cold, clear light.

HAWTHORN sits waiting for some friendly birds to come by. They love his juicy red berries.

The HOLLY Fairy is proud that his leaves stay green in winter, when most others turn brown. He parades his scarlet berries, knowing that they will soon be picked to make wreaths and other decorations to celebrate that most magical time—Christmas!

The beautiful SNOWDROP Fairy never feels the cold even though she is barefoot. She is a true winter fairy who loves the cold, crisp feel of snow and ice.

The bright yellow flowers of the WINTER JASMINE
Fairy bring a touch of golden cheer to the bleak winter
landscape.

The Winter is come, the cold winds blow;
I shall feel the frost and the drifting snow;
But the sun can shine in December too,
And this is the time of my gift to you.
See here, see here, my flowers appear!

ALMOND BLOSSOM'S SONG

Joy! the Winter's nearly gone!
Soon will Spring come dancing on;
And, before her, here dance I,
Pink like sunrise in the sky.
Other lovely things will follow;
Soon will cuckoo come, and swallow;
Birds will sing and buds will burst,
But the Almond is the first!

SECRET STORIES

ALMOND BLOSSOM'S MYSTERY

CHAPTER ONE
THE LONGEST WINTER

NONE OF THE FLOWER FAIRIES could remember winter ever being *this* long. The bitterly cold weather seemed to have gone on for an eternity. It was months since they'd opened their presents beneath the decorated boughs of the Christmas tree, while the rusty colors of autumn were just a distant memory. It wouldn't have been so bad if the sun was shining, but that was missing too, hidden behind a thick layer of dull cloud.

At first the Flower Fairies, who are usually very optimistic creatures, were hopeful that spring was just around the corner. But when the cold, dreary weather continued, they became puzzled. Finally they began to worry. Would it be winter forever? Without the sun, how would their garden flourish? Would the buds and blossoms never appear? The fairies whispered in hushed voices to each other, desperate to learn the answer to the most important question of all: *Where was spring?*

There was one Flower Fairy in particular who was very concerned about the long winter, and that was Almond Blossom. Day after day, she peered up at the grim, gray sky and then looked closely at the bare branches of her tree.

"Nothing," she sighed. "Not even a bud."

The pretty little fairy, no bigger than

a human hand, slumped despondently against the tree trunk.

Spring was the most important event on Almond Blossom's calendar. Every year, as soon as winter waved farewell, the milder weather encouraged her delicate pink blossoms to unfurl. For all the other Flower Fairies, this was the very first sign of spring. For Almond Blossom, it was her signal to perform the traditional dance that heralded the new season. She so enjoyed skipping and pirouetting around the garden, brandishing one of her own blossom-laden stems, to the sound of the delighted cheers of the other fairies. It just wouldn't be the same carrying a bare, brown twig.

"Cheer up!" called Sycamore from his lofty perch on a nearby tree. "Whatever you're thinking about might never happen!"

"That's what I'm worried about," Almond Blossom replied. "What if spring never happens—ever? What then?" Her pretty face crumpled and she sobbed great, fat tears of sorrow. "What'll I do? I may as well just pack up my things and leave the Flower Fairies Garden!"

Sycamore looked utterly horrified at the effect his seemingly harmless greeting had had on poor Almond Blossom, and he leaped the short distance between their trees, his gauzy wings glowing gold and green in the pale light. "There, there," he said, patting her shoulder awkwardly. Sycamore was at his happiest when fluttering and twirling through the air, a little like the winged seeds that whirled from his tree every autumn—he didn't have much experience in making glum fairies laugh. But he did his best.

"Spring *will* come," he said gently. "Just you wait and see."

"That's very kind of you, Sycamore," said Almond Blossom, wiping away her tears. She grabbed a dark green leaf and blew her nose into it noisily. "I don't know what's got into me. I think I might be missing the sun!" She laughed weakly.

Sycamore gave her an encouraging grin. "Soon it'll be so sunny that you'll wish for a cloud to come by to give you some shade!" he said.

But the dull, cloudy, cold weather continued. The only variation from the grayness was the occasional sharp shower that soaked and chilled any Flower Fairy unlucky enough to be out in the open.

Almond Blossom tried to keep her spirits up by practicing the steps of her spring dance, but her heart wasn't in it. Bleakly, she noticed that her fairy outfit was beginning to look very shabby. The pale pink petals of her tutu looked crumpled rather than frothy, while the ones adorning her chestnut locks were damp and bedraggled because of the rain. As for her dusky pink tunic, it had most definitely seen better days. Tansy—who was a whiz with needle and thread—offered to repair her clothes with some of Snowdrop's snowy white petals, but Almond Blossom politely refused.

44

It wouldn't feel right wearing someone else's petals. No, she would make herself a brand-new outfit when her own blossoms bloomed. Just as she did every year.

Then the crisis deepened. One murky morning, when the weather was so dark and gloomy that the Flower Fairies had to use pinches of precious fairy dust to light their way, word spread around the garden that an emergency meeting was to take place at the blackthorn bush.

As soon as she heard the news, Almond Blossom hopped down to the ground, smoothed her ragged clothes, and—peeping in a puddle on the way to make sure that she didn't look too scruffy—scurried toward the blackthorn bush. By the time she arrived, a large crowd of Flower Fairies had gathered. They muttered to each other in low voices.

"What's going on?" Almond Blossom asked Windflower, an elegant fairy with long, dark hair and mahogany-patterned wings.

Windflower shrugged. "I heard there was going to be some big announcement," she said. "But I haven't a clue what it's about."

"Shhhh!" whispered Blackthorn. She sat on a low branch, almost hidden by the tiny white flowers that smothered her plant—one of the very few to bear flowers in this chilly weather. "Someone's coming!"

"Greetings!" A powerful voice rang out, silencing the waiting crowd immediately. Heads swiveled round to see who had spoken, and then there was a collective gasp. A dazzling Flower Fairy stood before them. He was clothed in shimmering gold and wore a crown of yellow flower stamens on his golden hair. It was Kingcup—the king of the Flower Fairies! "Please be seated," the royal visitor continued.

Obediently, everyone sat.

Almond Blossom's throat was as dry as sandpaper, and she swallowed with difficulty. It didn't take a fairy diploma to know that bad news was coming.

"Flower Fairies . . . we have a problem," said Kingcup, his kind eyes clouded with concern. "I'm sure you've noticed that winter has gone on for a very long time. For some weeks, I was convinced that it was just an odd weather pattern and that any day we'd see dear Almond Blossom dancing merrily through the garden, followed swiftly by glorious spring weather." He paused to smile briefly at her. "But now I know different. Prepare yourselves, Flower Fairies, for the truth is shocking."

Everyone held their breath.

"Spring isn't late," said Kingcup. "*Spring has been stolen!*"

CHAPTER TWO
A GRAND PLAN

There was a stunned silence as the fairies absorbed the awful news. This wasn't the sort of thing that happened in the Flower Fairies Garden.

"I'm afraid there's more," said Kingcup apologetically. "Unfortunately, this year's Spring Party will have to be postponed . . . until spring is restored to its rightful place. I'm most terribly sorry."

There was a strangled sob in the middle of the crowd as one Flower Fairy was overwhelmed by the bad tidings.

Shakily, Almond Blossom raised an arm into the air. "If you please, sir . . ." she began.

Kingcup looked in her direction and nodded. "It's just that . . . er . . . what I-I-I'd like to know . . . that is, what I'm sure *everyone* w-would like to know is . . ." Almond Blossom paused, wishing that she felt braver. "How do you know? Why was spring stolen? Who did it? When? And where—"

"Whoa there," said Kingcup, his handsome face creasing into a brief smile. "Let me try to answer those questions before you think of any more." He reached into a pocket and pulled out a scroll of parchment tied with a long ribbon of grass. Slowly, thoughtfully, he held the parchment aloft. "This," he said, "is a ransom note. It explains everything—I think it's best if I read it aloud."

There were nods of approval from the crowd.

Dear Flower Fairies

My, what a long, cold winter! And do you know why? It's because we've stolen spring and hidden it from you. Ha ha! You'll never find it. But we're prepared to do a deal. In exchange for spring, we want six sacks filled to the brim with fairy dust.

On Saturday evening at sunset, you must leave these sacks beneath the almond tree. By Sunday morning, spring will return. No fairy dust means no spring.

Do not try to find us, or we will steal summer too.

Signed,

As if we'd tell you!

Kingcup rolled up the parchment and tucked it back into his pocket. "So, dear Flower Fairies," he said, "we have these dastardly thieves to thank for our worst ever winter. And now we need to work out what to do."

"Why that's simple!" piped up Rose, a friendly little fairy who loved to make others happy. "If everyone works extra hard, we should just about have enough fairy dust by Saturday. I have some large leaves that we could make into sturdy sacks. And perhaps the blackbirds would help by carrying the sacks from flower to flower until they are full."

"No way!" Sycamore cried indignantly. He leaped to his feet and looked stern. "We can't give in to their demands! We must send out a search party immediately and hunt high and low until we've tracked down the thieves."

"But then they'll steal summer!" wailed Daisy.

"I-I-I'm not sure we can make s-six sacks of f-fairy dust by S-S-Saturday." White Clover's round, rosy cheeks were awash with tears.

"We want to go to the Spring Party!" sobbed the Sweet Pea babies.

It was pandemonium. Everywhere Almond Blossom looked, there were Flower Fairies shouting or crying into their petal handkerchiefs. She looked around for Kingcup and saw that he was refereeing a squabble between Yew Fairy and Pine Tree Fairy. She scratched her head thoughtfully. If they were going to rescue spring *and* save the party, somebody needed to do something right now.

"*Please be quiet!*" bellowed Almond Blossom at the top of her voice. And everyone was so astonished by the mild-mannered fairy's command that they stopped shouting and arguing and crying immediately. "Thank you," she continued meekly. "I have a plan, if anyone would like to hear it?"

At once, a sea of heads nodded.

"Gather round," whispered Almond Blossom. "We don't want to be overheard."

By noon, it was settled. Most of the Flower Fairies would set to work making heaps of sparkling fairy dust. They decided it would be best if they obeyed the ransom letter's demands—or at least pretended to. Any enemy spies that might be lurking would be fooled into thinking that the fairies had given in. Meanwhile . . . Almond Blossom would search for spring!

"Aren't you even a tiny bit nervous?" asked Windflower, watching as Almond Blossom packed a small bag with fairy cheese, hazelnuts, and a nutcase filled with Elderberry's sweet juice.

Almond Blossom checked all around before nodding. "Oh yes!" she said. "But I'm excited too." It was true. She'd never done anything like this before—never been on a secret mission, never been trusted with such an important task. She could hardly wait!

"What will you do?" asked Windflower. "Where will you go?" Of all the Flower Fairies, she was perhaps the most eager for Almond Blossom to succeed, for her starlike, white flowers would appear when the first breeze of spring blew.

"First, I'm going to search the Flower Fairies Garden thoroughly," replied Almond Blossom, "just to make sure the thieves left no clues. Then I'll travel farther afield—and I won't stop until I've found spring." She smiled at Windflower as she shouldered her bag. "Don't worry—the blackbirds are going to fly above me. If I need help, I'll whistle for them."

"Take this," Windflower said hastily, thrusting a small, silky-soft bag into her friend's hand. "It's fairy dust. It's not much, I'm afraid, but it's all I have. Go on, run—and take care!" She leaped from the bare branch and somersaulted through the air, landing neatly on the ground below. "Farewell!" she cried, before hurrying away.

Almond Blossom smiled as she looked at Windflower's gift. Everybody was being so kind—she just hoped that she could repay them by returning with spring.

CHAPTER THREE
THE OUTSIDE WORLD

By the time Almond Blossom had finished exploring the Flower Fairies Garden, not a leaf or a stone or a fallen petal was left unturned. But she didn't find a single clue. Whoever had stolen spring had done a *very* good job of covering their tracks.

It's time to go over the wall, thought Almond Blossom, trudging toward the far side of the garden. Here, the wall backed onto open marshes, where only the occasional winding lane interrupted the wild countryside. Flower Fairies lived here too—among the reeds and wild grasses and nestling under flowers of the hedgerow and wayside. Many of these fairies visited the garden from time to time. Almond Blossom hoped to bump into them on her travels—it would be lovely to see a friendly face or two.

She gazed up at the ancient wall, relieved to see that there were plenty of hollows to slip her fingers and toes inside. Briskly, she climbed up the rough stones, stopping only when she reached the top.

"Phew!" said Almond Blossom, perching on the wall to admire the view. Far below her dangling feet was a wide, muddy track, its surface furrowed and uneven. Through the light mist that hung before her, she could make out a dark green hedgerow opposite. It was interwoven with bindweed—white, cushiony blooms that were bold enough and pushy enough to grow absolutely anywhere. She was wondering if White Bindweed Fairy was at home when a wisp of white mist engulfed her. Brrrr! She shivered at its cold touch. It seemed as if the rest of Flower Fairyland was in winter's steely grip too. Almond Blossom couldn't help feeling a little disappointed—she'd hoped that there might be a smidgen of warmth on the other side of the wall.

Ding ding! Ding-a-ling! Ding!

Abruptly, the silence of the quiet countryside was shattered by a frantic jangling of bells.

"Hurry up, Mark!" The anxious voice echoed along the track, accompanied by more *ding-a-ling*-ing. "We'll be late!"

"I'm coming!" replied another voice.

Humans! She'd never seen or heard one before, but others had told her how big and noisy they were. And according to Flower Fairy law, she *must* stay out of sight. If humans knew that fairies really did exist, the fairies' fragile world might be crushed underfoot by stampeding feet or harmed by curious fingers.

With nowhere to hide and no time to flee, Almond Blossom had no choice but to fold her wings shut and curl herself into the tightest possible ball.

And then she waited. The ground began to tremble horribly and there was an earsplitting screech. "I *really* need new brakes," muttered a voice. The Flower Fairy couldn't resist peeking and saw a girl with dark, silky hair and big blue eyes. She was crouching over a bright blue contraption that Almond Blossom knew must be a bicycle. The girl's face broke into a wide grin as a younger boy skidded to a halt beside her. They looked so much alike that they had to be sister and brother. "Where's Toby?" she asked.

"Not far away," replied the boy. "He was barking at some mushrooms a little way back. Oh, here he comes!"

A caramel-colored dog with floppy ears bounded out of the mist, sitting—*splat!*—in a puddle beside the children. He panted, his tongue lolling to one side.

I don't know what all the fuss is about, Almond Blossom thought to herself. *Humans seem perfectly harmless. Pleasant, even. And I rather like their d—*

Woof! Woof-woof! Toby the dog had begun to make the most awful racket that she'd ever heard. *Ow-ow-ow-WOOOOO!* he howled.

Almond Blossom's heart sank as, too late, she remembered how finely tuned animals' senses were. Now the dog was staring right at Almond Blossom. He'd seen her!

"What is it, Toby?" asked the boy. "You silly dog! There aren't any mushrooms up there . . . or *are* there?" He stood on tiptoe and squinted at the top of the wall.

Any second now, they would start clambering toward her, and then they would find her, and before nightfall she would be on display in a museum—Almond Blossom just knew it! Unless . . . Quickly, she delved her hand deep into the silken bag that Windflower had given her. She scooped a handful of the precious fairy dust into her palm and blew with all her might.

53

Whoosh!

A cloud of tiny pollen fragments billowed outward.

"Fairy dust, fairy dust, hide me from sight!" Almond Blossom whispered. At once, the air all around her began to glimmer and shimmer magically.

"What are you looking at, Mark?" asked the girl curiously.

"Er . . . nothing," replied her brother. "I could have sworn that I saw something . . ." He paused and frowned, scratching his head. "Something really strange. But now it's gone. I must have been mistaken."

Toby the dog had stopped barking now and was happily snuffling at the children's feet.

Almond Blossom smiled to herself. "Thank you, Windflower," she whispered in the tiniest of voices. The fairy dust had worked its magic brilliantly—she was *totally* shielded from view.

"Come on, then," said the girl. "Let's escape this murky weather—I want to see the sun again." She leaped back onto her bicycle. "Race you?"

As the children and their dog vanished around the corner, Almond Blossom rubbed her chin thoughtfully. Something was bothering her, but she couldn't for the life of her work out what it was.

CHAPTER FOUR
THE BIG ADVENTURE

Almond Blossom peered into the darkening gloom. This was not good. Night was falling and she hadn't even reached the marsh yet. And with only two days to go before Saturday's deadline, she didn't have a moment to lose. She grasped a piece of ivy that clung to the stone wall and expertly slid down its length, landing with a tiny *splish* on the sodden ground below.

Shouldering her bag once more, she skipped and fluttered across the track to the safety of the hedgerow.

"Yoohoo!" shouted White Bindweed, who was busy weaving flowers in and out of the hedge. "Are you staying for tea?"

"That's very kind of you," replied Almond Blossom, "but I can't stop. I'm searching for spring."

"Oh, I see . . ." said White Bindweed, screwing up her face as if she didn't really see at all. She shrugged and grinned. "Okay, then. Catch you later!"

Almond Blossom fought her way through the hedge, which for someone as small as a Flower Fairy was more like a huge and very spooky forbidden forest. Sturdy branches blocked her path, while twigs sprang at her and tore her already tattered clothes. And it was *so* dark. Bravely she pushed on,

reminding herself that the happiness of the Flower Fairies *and* the magnificent Spring Party were at stake. She *had* to succeed.

At last, she reached the other side of the hedge. The overcast sky was charcoal gray now—soon it would be black—but there was just enough light for Almond Blossom to see a little way. She plunked herself down on a handy rock and admired the view. So this was the fabled marsh. A carpet of moss stretched away from her, dotted with clumps of tall grass. Large, lumpy shapes loomed in the distance. For a moment, she feared they might be giants or ogres or some other scary creatures, but then she realized that they were probably just trees. She giggled to herself, as excitement fizzed through her once more. This was a grand adventure, all right.

"Time to go!" she announced to the empty wilderness. She leaped to her feet and marched away from the hedge, trying hard not to lose her balance on the springy moss.

Almond Blossom soon learned that while the Flower Fairies Garden was quite flat, the marsh was a totally different story. Hollows nestled between grassy hillocks, some of which were mountainous. She struggled to the top of the highest of these mounds, deciding that it would be a perfect spot to camp for the night. But when she reached the top, all thoughts of sleep instantly vanished from her mind.

"What *is* it?" breathed the little Flower Fairy. A bright stripe of sparkling color split the darkness, stretching from left to right across the distant horizon. Almond Blossom had never seen anything so wonderful. It glittered like the brightest jewel and burned as bright as the biggest candle. It was vivid pink and luscious orange and deepest mauve.

It was beautiful.

But she still didn't know what it *was*. Dazzled and bewildered, Almond Blossom sank onto the comfortable moss and stared. Little by little, the mysterious glow faded from view, the colors darkening, the light dimming . . . until it was gone. Then, tired beyond belief, she slept.

"Wakey, wakey, rise and shine!" sang a friendly voice.

"Hmmm?" groaned Almond Blossom. She looked up groggily to see two of the scruffiest Flower Fairies she'd ever laid eyes on staring down at her. "Who are you?" she asked.

"I'm Rush-Grass," announced the dark-haired fairy. He reached down to shake Almond Blossom's hand, pumping it up and down enthusiastically. "Pleased to meet you."

"And I'm Cotton-Grass," said the other fairy, with a cheeky grin. His hair was ash blond and stood up from his head as if he'd had a very big fright. "We're brothers."

Almond Blossom smiled back, noticing absentmindedly that the two Flower Fairies had *very* pointy ears. And although their wings were quite plain, their clothes blended in perfectly with the colors of the marsh grasses—chestnut brown, moss green, and deep maroon. In fact, they seemed so much at home on the marsh that she knew without asking that they must be locals.

"You're not from around here, are you?" said Rush-Grass, reminding her that she hadn't introduced herself yet.

"Oh, I'm sorry," she said. "How very rude of me. I'm Almond Blossom— I come from the Flower Fairies Garden." She sprang to her feet and curtsied politely.

"There's no need for that," said Cotton-Grass, with a stifled giggle. "You're on the marsh now—we're much more laid back here than the fairies in your garden." He gave his brother a sideways glance. "Are *you* going to ask her?"

Rush-Grass nodded. "What are you *doing* here?" he asked curiously. "Are you lost? Because if you're lost, we'd be delighted to lead you to safety. That's our job, you see."

Almond Blossom shook her head.

"And if you're *not* lost," added Cotton-Grass, "then we're pretty good guides too. We can show you all the sights—the twisty marsh path, the fairy rings, the elves' secret hideaway, Mallow's famous fairy cheese—"

"What?" Almond Blossom spluttered. Of course! How could she have been so forgetful?

"It's delicious," said Cotton-Grass, rubbing his tummy and making *mmmmm* noises. "Mallow's seeds make the most excellent cheese—the best in Flower Fairyland—"

"No, not the *cheese*," interrupted Almond Blossom again. "The elves! Can you help me to find them?"

"But of course," replied Rush-Grass. He gave an exasperated sigh and rolled his eyes. "What have they done now?" he asked.

"Well, they may have done *nothing*," began Almond Blossom uncertainly. She was a very fair fairy and liked to give everyone a chance, but the elves were well known throughout the Flower Fairies Garden for their tricks and monkey business. Stealing spring would be just the sort of mischief they loved. "I have a feeling that they might be able to point me in the right direction," she added.

Noticing that the brothers were looking quite confused, Almond Blossom told them how the Flower Fairies had received a ransom note and there were no clues in their garden, so she'd ventured over the wall and onto the marsh to search for any sign of spring or the wicked thieves who'd stolen it. "Surely you must have noticed how long winter has lasted?" she said.

"Oh, yes," said Cotton-Grass. "The weather's dreadful here, isn't it?" He looked up at the thick gray clouds above them. "It's much nicer on the other side of the marsh. We should take you there." He pointed. "Look!"

Almond Blossom looked. She blinked. Then she looked again. There, in the distance, was a sunny strip of yellow, just visible at the edge of the low gray cloud. Was it . . .? Could it really be . . .? It was!

"Hurray!" she cheered, fluttering into the air with joy. "It's springtime! We've found *spring*!"

CHAPTER FIVE
CAUGHT

———————

At once, everything slotted into place ... Spring hadn't been stolen—it was simply hidden behind a thick blanket of gray cloud. This explained why the children had hurried to escape the murky weather and find the sun. It also explained why it seemed as if winter had lasted so long this year.

"The beautiful stripe of color was the sunset," breathed Almond Blossom. It was such an age since she'd seen the evening sun, she'd forgotten how magnificent it could be. She was so pleased that she couldn't resist a happy skip and a hop, much to the delight of her new fairy friends.

Then she sat down and thought. And thought. But no matter how she puzzled and pondered, mused and mulled it over, she kept coming back to the same conclusion. Whoever had sent the ransom note to the Flower Fairies must *also* have hung the great dark cloud above their garden.

"Will you help me to find the thieves?" she asked the marsh fairies. "I want to ask the elves what they know, but I don't know where to find them."

Rush-Grass and Cotton-Grass nodded solemnly.

"We'll take you there as soon as you've had breakfast," said Rush-Grass sensibly. "It's really not a good idea to do this sort of thing on an empty stomach."

So as soon as Almond Blossom had nibbled a hazelnut and sipped the cool spring water that Cotton-Grass had brought her, they set off across the marsh. They trekked past tall, waving grasses and around squidgy bogs, the two brothers making sure that she didn't stray away from the path and into danger.

It didn't take long to reach the edge of the cloud, where the marsh was bathed in glorious sunshine. Almond Blossom paused for a moment, closing her eyes and raising her face up to the gentle warmth of the sun.

"There," Cotton-Grass whispered.

Almond Blossom blinked a little as her eyes got used to the brightness. "Where?" she whispered back, scanning the area all around them.

Cotton-Grass pointed to an innocent-looking cluster of toadstools a short distance away.

They were quite the prettiest things Almond Blossom had seen all morning, with their chocolatey-brown stems and their cherry-red caps, dotted all over with large white spots. The colors dazzled in the spring sunshine.

"Quite poisonous, of course," muttered Rush-Grass. "And the perfect place for those naughty elves to hide their secret headquarters."

"We don't *know* that they've done anything wrong," said Almond Blossom.

"Hmmm." Cotton-Grass didn't sound so sure. "Then let's go and find out," he said, marching toward the toadstools. But before they even reached the elves' secret hideaway, gleeful voices rang out loud and clear.

"We've *fooled* them!"

"Tomorrow we'll have *six sacks* of fairy dust!"

"We are *so* clever! Ha ha *haaa*!"

Almond Blossom crept closer and peered between the toadstools. And there, in a small clearing, were three green-clad creatures with pointy ears and pointy wings. They were laughing fit to burst. "You're not that clever," she said sweetly.

The elves spun around. "Oh," said the tallest of the three.

"Oh, indeed," said Almond Blossom, squeezing through a narrow gap into the hideaway. She put her hands on her hips and frowned at the guilty-looking trio. "Why did you do it?" she asked.

"We only wanted some fairy dust," mumbled the shortest elf, staring down at his feet. "It's not fair, you know," he said. "You Flower Fairies have all the fun, with your singing and dancing in your *wonderful* garden."

He looked up and glared at Almond Blossom, who was suddenly feeling a little sorry for the miserable creatures.

"We thought it would be funny if we were enjoying the lovely spring weather, while you were stuck under a wintry cloud," he continued. "And it *was* funny. We haven't been able to *stop* laughing." He looked at his two sidekicks. "Have we, lads?"

"Er, yes . . ." said the tall elf quickly. "I mean, no, boss."

"Ho ho ho," the third elf laughed unconvincingly. "Hee hee."

"But why did you write the ransom note?" asked Almond Blossom, curious now. "Why didn't you just hide the sun and be done with it? Why did you want the fairy dust too? Elves have their own magic dust, don't they?"

"It's not as sparkly as yours," grumbled the chief elf. "And it's not quite as magical either. Besides, we've only got about a thimbleful left—it took heaps of elf dust to cast the Winter Cloud Spell." He paused and looked suddenly cunning. "Why don't you tell us how to make fairy dust? Because if we knew how to make it, we wouldn't need yours, would we?"

"Nice try!" Almond Blossom laughed. "But I'm afraid that only Flower Fairies can make fairy dust—and how we make it is a closely guarded secret."

"Hmmmph," said the elf.

Almond Blossom thought deeply. Here was a problem indeed. How was she to convince the elves to lift the cloud that covered the Flower Fairies Garden *without* collecting the six sacks of fairy dust they'd demanded? Unless . . .

Almond Blossom pulled out the silky bag that Windflower had given her.

"Listen very carefully," she said mysteriously. "I have an idea."

Chapter Six
Back to the Garden

Almond Blossom ran her fingertips over her velvet-soft tunic and gently touched the tiny petals sewn around the neck. Then she whirled around, grinning with delight as the pink petals of her skirt spun outward. Her new outfit was perfect.

She was ready.

Carefully breaking off a twig from her tree—she made sure to choose one that was heavily laden with brand-new blossoms—Almond Blossom clutched it tightly before leaping into the air. Gracefully, she fluttered downward, landing lightly far below, where green shoots were beginning to poke through the soil.

Almond Blossom raised herself on tiptoes, took a deep breath, and began to sing the words that the Flower Fairies had waited so long to hear:

"Joy! The Winter's nearly gone!
Soon will Spring come dancing on;
And before her, here dance I,
Pink like sunrise in the sky.
Other lovely things will follow;
Soon will cuckoo come, and swallow;
Birds will sing and buds will burst,
But the Almond is the first!"

Happily, she danced through the garden, twirling and high-stepping as she went, hopping and leaping, spinning and swaying.

"Almond Blossom!" cried Sycamore as she jigged past. "Am I glad to see you! Does this mean that spring is officially on the way?" In reply, she pointed to the east, where the early morning sun was rising above the horizon, turning the wispy clouds above them the same shade of pink as her pretty blossoms.

"Hurray!" cheered Sycamore, bouncing up and down on a branch. Then he stopped. "But what happened to the nasty winter weather? Did we pay the ransom?"

"Oh, I don't think so," Almond Blossom said gaily. "There must be something in the air, I suppose." She waved her flowery twig. "Must dash! Don't forget about the Spring Party!" She chuckled gleefully as she danced away, leaving a stunned Sycamore behind her.

Everything had turned out so well. Understandably, the elves had been dubious about her idea at first. They were utterly dazzled by the expectation of the six wonderful sacks of magical fairy dust that awaited them, and they were unwilling to give them up. But Almond Blossom had made them feel so guilty with stories of the heartbroken Flower Fairies with tears dripping down their cheeks as they pined for spring that they gave in at last and agreed to lift the Winter Cloud Spell. Because their stocks of elf dust were so low, Almond Blossom had handed over the little silken bag—there were still a couple of handfuls of Windflower's precious fairy dust left—and made the elves promise to use it wisely, before she hitched a lift home with a friendly blackbird.

Now, as she admired the glorious morning sky, Almond Blossom saw that the elves had kept their word.

"Joy! The winter's nearly gone!" she sang again, continuing her merry dance.

The Flower Fairies were so eager for the new season to arrive that the Spring Party was held only a few days later. The garden was decked with as many flowers as Almond Blossom could spare and bunches of sunny yellow daffodils. Wildflower's tiny white flowers were scattered over the ground like fallen stars, while swathes of newly opened bluebells stretched as far as the eye could see. So much extra fairy dust had been made that week, it was sprinkled here and there. The glade gleamed and twinkled everywhere the Flower Fairies looked.

It was a wonderful party. Lots of familiar faces joined in the fun, but there were some unfamiliar faces too. Rush-Grass and Cotton-Grass had made the long journey across the marsh—they turned out to be excellent dancers—and three more visitors weren't far behind.

The elves smiled sheepishly at Almond Blossom as they sipped Elderberry's famous juice from buttercups. "Thank you for inviting us," mumbled the chief elf, fiddling with his cuff.

"We love to dance," said the second elf, who was unable to stop his feet from tapping.

"We just never get the chance," said the third elf. "Thank you."

"It's the least I could do," Almond Blossom replied. "After all, you did return spring to us!"

And with that she winked at the elves and fluttered across to join her fairy friends at her favorite party of the year.

PINK FAIRIES' SONG

Early in the mornings,
when children still are sleeping,
Or late, late at night-time,
beneath the summer moon,
What are they doing,
the busy fairy people?
Could you creep to spy them,
in silent magic shoon.

You might learn a secret,
among the garden borders,
Something never guessed at,
that no one knows or thinks:
Snip, snip, snip go busy fairy scissors,
Pinking out the edges
of the petals of the Pinks!

Fairies at Work and Play

ALL FLOWER FAIRIES work very hard looking after the plants, flowers, and trees around them. They sweep away dead leaves and polish up new ones. They keep their flowers shaped, clean, and tidy. And every Flower Fairy helps with the important job of sowing seeds and watering the new seedlings.

Flower Fairies like to keep their homes clean, so housework is very important to them. Their beds, with tiny sheets of petals and leaves, are freshly made each morning, and the floors are swept with tall grasses.

Dainty Shirley Poppy helps to sow seeds.

Some fairies have special jobs to do, all of which help plants or other fairies in some way. Whichever task they perform, all the fairies enjoy their work and look forward to each new day.

Flower Fairies also make sure that there is time each day to relax, play, and have fun. This may involve playing hide-and-seek, dancing, singing, or simply relaxing by a plant with a cup of jasmine tea!

The Pink Fairies use tiny scissors to give their flowers a distinctive look!

Black Medick looks after the seed heads.

THE FAIRIES' BUSY DAY

Flower Fairies rise with the sunshine, as there is always lots to be done. Once they have cleaned their homes and tended to their plants it is time to get on with the day's jobs. Each Flower Fairy has a special talent that he or she loves to put to good use. Some fairies do practical things, such as looking after the fairy children, washing clothes, or preparing fairy food.

Other fairies make fragrant scents from their crushed petals or create beautiful outfits from leaves and flowers. When dusk falls most fairies go to bed, but the night fairies, who have been asleep all day, stay awake to look after the plants and flowers.

You will need:

Scraps of fabric
such as cotton or silk

Ruler

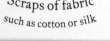

Pinking shears

Fabric glue

Paintbrush

Teaspoon

Lavender seeds

Ribbon

Buttons to decorate

LAVENDER'S SCENTED SACHETS

Lavender's flowers make the Flower Fairies Garden smell beautiful. These pretty scented sachets will keep your clothes smelling sweet!

1. Use pinking shears to cut your fabric into a rectangular strip, 3 inches wide and 10 inches long.

2. On the prettier side of the fabric, paint a thin strip of fabric glue down each long edge.

3. Carefully fold the fabric in half, pressing the long side edges together, and leave the glue to dry.

4. Turn the fabric inside out. Gently push the handle of a teaspoon into the corners to neaten the shape.

Place the bag in your clothes drawers or under your pillow.

Lavender's craft tip

If you have lavender growing in your garden, you can gather the seeds yourself. Pick the lavender heads when in full bloom, leave the heads to dry, and then remove the scented seeds.

5. Fill your bag with lavender seeds, leaving around 2 inches of fabric free at the top.

6. When the bag is nearly full, tie a pretty ribbon in a bow tightly around its neck.

Why not sew pretty buttons or lace on to your lavender bag?

TANSY THE FAIRY TAILOR

TANSY'S cutting and stitching is the best in the fairy world, so, naturally, she has the job of making the fairies' beautiful clothes. She uses a needle from a pine tree, and her thread is made from dried grass. When Tansy makes a new outfit she asks the fairies to collect their own materials for the costume. Once she has the petals and leaves she works hard to create a wonderful new garment. The tiny round flowers of her plant make lovely buttons!

Tansy also does mending, and she is so good at it that her repairs are practically invisible. If a Flower Fairy's dress needs patching, or her skirt is ripped, she will pick a petal or leaf from her plant and take it to Tansy, who will make it look good as new.

Were ever such button-like flowers seen—
Yellow, for elfin coats of green?
Three in a row—I stitch them so!

BUGLE THE FAIRY GUARD

BUGLE has extremely sensitive hearing, and he makes use of this skill in his job as guard for the fairy world. Still and quiet, he stands watching, looking out for signs of danger—particularly the sound of approaching humans! If all is clear, he lifts the blue bugle from his side and blows it loud and long. The deep trumpeting penetrates the woods and gardens nearby and tells the fairies it is safe to come out. All the Flower Fairies feel secure when Bugle is around.

At the edge of the woodland
Where good fairies dwell,
Stands, on the lookout,
A brave sentinel.

At the call of his bugle
Out the elves run,
Ready for anything,
Danger, or fun,
Hunting, or warfare,
By moonshine or sun.

Self-Heal the Fairy Nurse

SELF-HEAL is the caring nurse of the Flower Fairy world. Any fairy who has been hurt or injured will soon get a visit from this kind fairy. She gets to work right away, administering medicinal herbs and gently wrapping injured limbs in tiny bandages. Cuts and scratches are common among fairies, and occasionally a Flower Fairy will doze off and fall to the ground. This is particularly painful for treetop fairies! But everyone who is treated by Self-Heal soon feels much better. And she doesn't treat just fairies—she tends to all the creatures of the wood. So if you ever spot a frog or a mouse wearing a tiny bandage, you'll
know who has helped it!

When little elves have cut themselves,
Or Mouse has hurt her tail,
Or Froggie's arm has come to harm,
This herb will never fail.
The Fairy's skill can cure each ill
And soothe the sorest pain;
She'll bathe and bind,
and soon they'll find
That they are well again.

PLAYFUL FAIRIES

There's always work for the Flower Fairies
to do, but there's plenty of time to have fun too.
All fairies love games and playing, music and dancing.
And there is much fun to be had among the gardens,
hedgerows, woods, and trees of the fairy world. Hide-
and-seek is one of the fairies' favorite games, and, as they
are used to hiding from humans, they are extremely good at it!

MUSIC AND DANCING

Flower Fairies love to celebrate with music and dancing. They have wonderful singing voices and will burst into song at any opportunity. Many of them can also play instruments: fairies such as BLUEBELL and HAREBELL have hundreds of bells on their flowers to ring, while the grass fairies play merry tunes on tiny flutes fashioned from hollow reeds.

Those fairies without instruments simply clap their hands along to the music and skip around. The CROCUS Fairies are renowned for their beautiful dancing, and they always get a round of applause from their appreciative fairy friends.

A Room in Bloom

The PINK FAIRIES like to make very special party decorations. With a little snip here and some pretty tissue paper there, they can turn any room into a beautiful chamber.

Tissue Carnations

1. Take five sheets of double-ply tissue paper and separate them so that you have ten pieces of thin tissue.

2. Put the sheets on top of each other, and ask an adult to help you cut off the edges and corners to create a circular shape.

3. Scrunch the tissue into a ball, then open it up again. To create the flower, pinch the tissues beneath the center of the pile and twist slightly. Secure with a piece of tape.

4. Fluff out the petals to complete your decoration.

You will need:

Pink, yellow, or white tissue paper (double-ply)
Tape
Scissors

DRESS-UP NAME CARDS

1. For each of your guests, cut out a square of card that is approximately 3 by 3 inches. Holding the card vertically, fold up the bottom 1 inch to form a stand.

2. Draw a simple fairy shape on to your card. Leave a little room somewhere to add the name of your guest.

3. Ask an adult to help you cut different squares of fabric to create an outfit for each fairy. Try to choose colors or styles to suit each guest!

4. Decorate with sequins or glitter.

5. Use colored pencils or markers to color in your fairy and write each guest's name.

You will need:
White card
Colored pencils
or markers
Scissors
Ruler
Glitter or sequins
Fabric
Fabric glue

PANSY'S CHAIR WINGS

You will need:
1 piece of
poster board
Blue, yellow, and
purple paint
String
Scissors

1. Fold the poster board in half vertically. When folded, it should be about as wide as your back.

2. Draw a wing along the folded edge— just like drawing half a butterfly.

3. Cut around the edge of the wing and open it out to make a butterfly shape.

4. Decorate the wings by using very watery paint and gentle brush strokes. Let the paints run together to look like Pansy's wings!

5. When the wings are dry, ask an adult to help you make two holes in the middle, about 1 inch apart, and thread the ends of a piece of string through. Use this string to tie your wings to the back of each guest's chair.

Make a set of wings for each guest. Now when you sit down to eat, you will all have fairy wings!

Parties and Balls

Flower Fairies have lots to celebrate, and many balls and parties are held throughout the year. These take place deep in the forests and woods and at the bottom of the garden, where humans cannot overhear the celebrations!

When the fairies hear CANTERBURY BELL's flowers ringing, they know a party is about to start, and so fairies from far and wide begin to gather. The fairy children love to see the beautiful dresses that the older fairies wear to the ball. They dream of the day they will be old enough to wear such gorgeous gowns!

At the party, the singing and dancing go on late into the night, and the next day there are always lots of sleepy fairies dozing under their plants!

Four times a year the fairies throw a special ball to celebrate the beginning of the new season.

Party Games

The ELDER FAIRY loves to make up fairy party games. Here are some ideas for your party. Her special tip is to think of all your favorite games and then give them a special fairy touch!

Fairy Treasure

You need two players or two teams. Write a list of clues to place around the house or garden. Color-code these clues for each team. Number each one, and ask the teams to find each one in order until they reach the Fairy Treasure! If you want to join in with this game, you'll have to ask an adult to write and hide the clues.

Musical Flowers

Place some giant paper flower shapes all over the floor. Use one less shape than the number of players. Start the music. All players show their best fairy moves. If the music is loud, they dance quickly; and if the music is quiet, they dance slowly. When the music stops, each fairy must find a flower to jump on. Take away a flower each time a fairy is "out." The fairy left standing is the winner!

86

Guessing Game
Mystery Guest

One player pretends to
be a creature found in the garden,
and the others each take turns to ask a
question that can only be answered
with "Yes" or "No." Carry on until the name
of the creature is revealed!

Ideas for garden creatures:
butterfly, ladybird, beetle, blackbird,
robin. (And don't forget—fairy!)

Smiling Game
Oh, Pretty Fairy

Sit in a circle with one player in
the middle. The player in the
middle goes to anyone in the circle and
says: "Oh, pretty fairy, won't you give me a
smile?" The player replies: "Sorry, pretty fairy,
but I just can't smile," and keeps a straight face!
The player in the middle can do anything to make
the other players smile except touch them.
The first person to smile swaps places
and goes in the middle.

Fairies and fun—they're one
and the same,
And there's never more fun
than in party games!

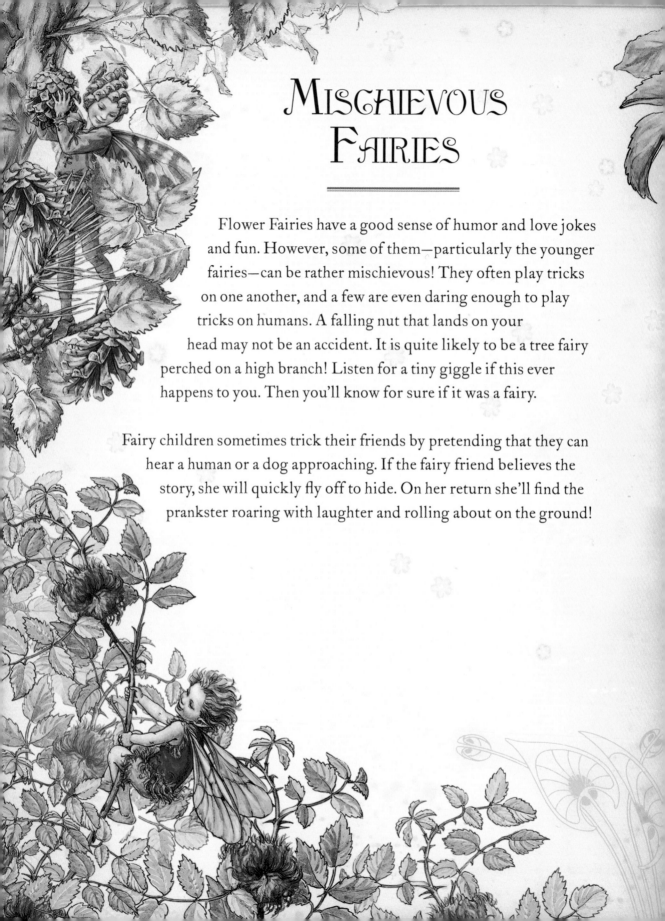

Mischievous Fairies

Flower Fairies have a good sense of humor and love jokes
and fun. However, some of them—particularly the younger
fairies—can be rather mischievous! They often play tricks
on one another, and a few are even daring enough to play
tricks on humans. A falling nut that lands on your
head may not be an accident. It is quite likely to be a tree fairy
perched on a high branch! Listen for a tiny giggle if this ever
happens to you. Then you'll know for sure if it was a fairy.

Fairy children sometimes trick their friends by pretending that they can
hear a human or a dog approaching. If the fairy friend believes the
story, she will quickly fly off to hide. On her return she'll find the
prankster roaring with laughter and rolling about on the ground!

When the nuts are falling fast,
Thrown by little me—
Tiny things to patter down
From a forest tree!

Under trees and in other shady places,
PERIWINKLE spreads his blue flowers
and dark green leaves. When he's feeling
mischievous, he uses the prickly edges
around his leaves to tickle the
other fairies' feet!

LILAC FAIRY'S SONG

White May is flowering,
Red May beside;
Laburnum is showering
Gold far and wide;
But I sing of Lilac,
The dearly-loved Lilac,
Lilac, in Maytime
A joy and a pride!

I love her so much
That I never can tell
If she's sweeter to look at,
Or sweeter to smell.

Fairy Flowers and Trees

FLOWERS, TREES, and other plants are very important to Flower Fairies. They have a special relationship because one cannot exist without the other; a fairy can only be born when a new seed sprouts. Flower Fairy babies sleep hidden under their plants' leaves, and they grow as the plant grows. The fairy lives with his or her special flower or tree forever.

It is a fairy's responsibility to care for her plant, a job which she loves doing. She will stay close to it as much as possible (leaving only occasionally for trips to other fairies' homes and to attend parties or markets).

She keeps her plant strong and healthy by making sure it has plenty of sunshine to bask in and water to drink, and by cleaning and polishing its flowers and stems. You will often find a fairy singing a special song to her plant while she goes about her work.

Flowers and trees provide the fairies with everything they need: homes, shelter, clothes, food, and places to play. The petals and leaves are used for clothes, which help disguise the fairies, and they also make beautiful decorations and fairy jewelery.

You will need:

Pretty silky fabric
in your favorite colors

Ruler

Pencil

Pinking shears

Scissors

Drinking straws
cut into 1 inch lengths

String, wool, or
embroidery thread

CANDYTUFT'S GARLAND

Be a fairy queen for the day by making this gorgeous garland to wear around your neck. You could make a tiny garland bracelet too!

1. Fold a piece of fabric 20 inches x 20 inches in half, then in half again. Make a template as shown opposite. Draw around it 24 times on to the fabric.

2. Ask an adult to help you cut out the flowers with the pinking shears. Hold the fabric tightly as you cut it so it doesn't slip. Separate each flower.

3. Repeat steps one and two using a smaller piece of different fabric (10 inches x 10 inches) and drawing only eight flower shapes.

4. Fold each flower in half, then in half again. Now snip a tiny triangle out of the point of the material using your scissors.

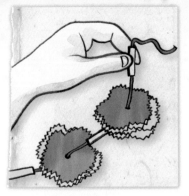

5. Arrange the flowers in layers. Each flower in this garland has three layers of pale lilac and one layer of purple fabric.

6. Thread the flower groups together, divided by the straw pieces. When the garland is as long as you want it, knot the end of the thread.

Don't worry if you don't cut out perfectly shaped flowers— you won't notice when they are strung together in the garland!

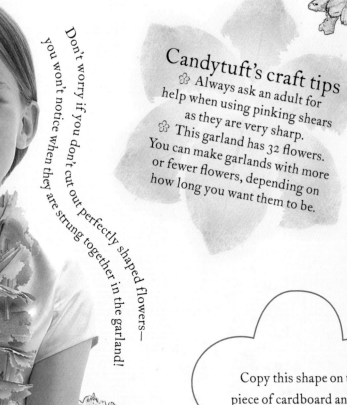

Candytuft's craft tips
❁ Always ask an adult for help when using pinking shears as they are very sharp.
❁ This garland has 32 flowers. You can make garlands with more or fewer flowers, depending on how long you want them to be.

Copy this shape on to a piece of cardboard and cut it out to make a template.

THE MEANINGS OF FLOWERS

The Flower Fairies know that many of their flowers and plants have special meanings. Some are magical, others have unique qualities, and some have stories or legends associated with them. Here are some of the fairies' favorites:

SECRETS OF THE DAISY

❀ The daisy is very sensitive to the sun, opening its petals as soon as the sun rises and closing them again when evening comes. This habit gives the flower its name: day's eye.

❀ Daisies are associated with children because of their simplicity and innocence and also because children love to make daisy chains with them.

❀ According to folklore, if a young girl picks a bunch of daisies with her eyes shut, the number of flowers she picks represents the number of years that will pass before she gets married.

Secrets of the Honeysuckle

❀ This lovely flower is celebrated for its sweet scent, which can perfume an entire garden on a still night. The honeysuckle plant clings as it grows, and this has made it into a symbol of everlasting love and faithfulness.

❀ In folklore, honeysuckle brought into the house is a sign that a wedding will happen in the future. A vase of its flowers put in a girl's bedroom is said to make her dream of love.

❀ The name *honeysuckle* comes from the fact that bees have to crawl right inside the trumpet of the flower in order to feed on the sweet nectar within.

Pretty fresh flowers

Scissors

Paper towels

Heavy books

PANSY'S PRESSED FLOWERS

Pansy loves her beautiful, vibrant flowers, and they look just as stunning when they are pressed!

1. Pick flowers that are about to bloom or have just opened. Cut off stems just below the flower heads.

2. Carefully space your flower heads out on a paper towel. Try to keep the petals flat.

3. Place another paper towel on top, then place the sheets between the pages of a large book.

4. Put the book in a safe place so it won't be disturbed, then pile several heavy books on top.

Dried flowers

It's easy to dry bunches of garden flowers such as lavender or sweetly scented rosebuds.

Tie string around the stems. Hang the flowers upside down in a warm, dry place until they are dry. You could put some dried flower heads in a bowl and add a few drops of lavender oil for some pretty, sweet-smelling potpourri.

5. Leave the flowers for one week, then transfer them to fresh paper towels. Press for another week.

6. Carefully remove the flowers. You can use your flowers to decorate cards or pretty gift tags.

Pansy's craft tips
❀ Daisies, buttercups, violets, fuchsia, lavender and pansies are among the best flowers to press.
❀ Keep picked flowers in water in the fridge until you are ready to press them.

99

THE MEANINGS
OF TREES

Every tree has its own group of Flower Fairies, who live
high up among its branches and leaves. The fairies adore
their beautiful trees and know all about their special
meanings and qualities:

SECRETS OF THE
MOUNTAIN ASH

❀ The mountain ash, or rowan tree, was once
known as the witch-wood tree. It was believed
to be a protection against witchcraft, and people
would sometimes carry a piece of mountain
ash in their pocket, for this reason.

❀ Its name comes from the old Norse
word *runa*, which means "charm."

❀ Ancient peoples believed
that the rowan was magical and
used its wood to foretell the future.

To English folk the mighty oak
Is England's noblest tree;
Its hard-grained wood is strong and good
As English hearts can be.

Secrets of the Oak Tree

❀ The oak is known as the king of the woods
and is believed to represent the spirit of England.
Its qualities are those associated with kings:
mighty, strong, and noble.

❀ Oak trees can live for many hundreds of years and
are renowned for their long lives and endurance.

❀ In folklore it is believed that the oak tree
helps in difficult times by bringing strength,
faith, and courage to those who sit beneath it.

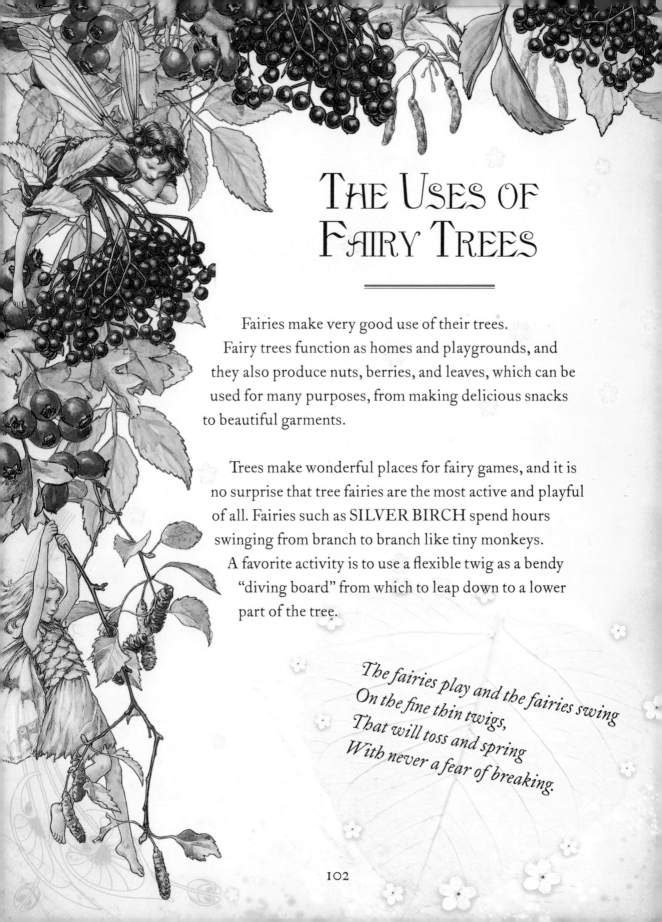

THE USES OF FAIRY TREES

Fairies make very good use of their trees.
Fairy trees function as homes and playgrounds, and
they also produce nuts, berries, and leaves, which can be
used for many purposes, from making delicious snacks
to beautiful garments.

Trees make wonderful places for fairy games, and it is
no surprise that tree fairies are the most active and playful
of all. Fairies such as SILVER BIRCH spend hours
swinging from branch to branch like tiny monkeys.
A favorite activity is to use a flexible twig as a bendy
"diving board" from which to leap down to a lower
part of the tree.

The fairies play and the fairies swing
On the fine thin twigs,
That will toss and spring
With never a fear of breaking.

Hollowed-out pinecones make terrific hats,
but the PINE TREE Fairy has just found another
use for them—in a game with the squirrels!

The elves play games with the squirrels
At the top of the tall, tall tree
Throwing cones for the squirrels to nibble—
I wish I were there to see!

Little POPLAR pretends that his soft
white fluff is snow and lets it gently drift about.
But it has a practical use too—as stuffing for the
fairies' pillows and cushions. No wonder their
beds are so comfortable!

GORSE FAIRIES' SONG

'When gorse is out of blossom,'
　　(Its prickles bare of gold)
'Then kissing's out of fashion,'
　　Said country-folk of old.
Now Gorse is in its glory
　　In May when skies are blue,
But when its time is over,
　　Whatever shall we do?

O dreary would the world be,
　　With everyone grown cold—
Forlorn as prickly bushes
　　Without their fairy gold!
But this will never happen:
　　At every time of year
You'll find one bit of blossom—
　　A kiss from someone dear!

Fairy Friends and Families

FRIENDS are very important to Flower Fairies, as they enjoy the company of other fairies and they love to talk, play, and have fun.

Some fairies, like CANDYTUFT, like to spend time with a group of friends. Others, like SNAPDRAGON, prefer to have one special friend. To a Flower Fairy, it's not important how many friends she has but how much they mean to her.

What Flower Fairies never forget is that no one should ever feel left out. If they see a fairy looking a bit lonely, they'll rush over at once. That's what being a Flower Fairy is all about!

*A fairy friend will change your frown
into a smile when you are down.*

Friends always help each other out, and this is
certainly true in the fairy world. If a fairy needs a
particular ingredient for a cake she is baking or a
helping hand with the housework, one of her friends
is sure to lend a hand.

Water fairy IRIS is a good friend to all the fairies,
because she teaches them how to swim,
even if they are afraid of water. Her best
friend is the tiny FORGET-ME-NOT,
who looks up to tall, graceful Iris.

Making New Friends

Flower Fairies find it easy to make new friends, and they like to get to know fairies from other parts of the fairy world. For example, a garden fairy might befriend a water fairy, or a tree fairy might drop in on a grass fairy. It gives them an opportunity to find out about other ways of living and to exchange useful ideas or recipes.

Fairies are very polite and will always bring a gift if visiting a friend for tea. This will usually be something the fairy has made herself, such as fragrant perfume made from her own petals or a freshly baked fairy cake.

It makes me feel so happy,
To make a brand-new friend,
The best of you, the best of me,
Is such a special blend.

ANIMAL FRIENDS

Fairies not only look after each other, they also try to help the many creatures that live close to them in the woods and gardens. Animals, birds, and insects all benefit from fairy treats, and they think themselves lucky to have such good fairy friends.

RED CLOVER
cares for the bumblebees.
In return they give the
fairies delicious honey
to share!

When caterpillars first change into
butterflies, they are very surprised.
Fairies often find new butterflies
sitting on flowers wondering what to do
next. MICHAELMAS DAISY tells them
how to flap their wings
and take to the air.

Snails are not always
popular with fairies
because they snack on leaves
and flowers. Luckily, snails are
sleepy creatures and can be easily
encouraged to nod off so that
they forget all about
eating.

RIBWORT PLANTAIN
is a wonderful whistler.
His tunes can soothe even
the hungriest snail
to sleep!

SELF-HEAL is the nurse of
the Flower Fairy world. If any
fairies or animals hurt themselves,
they pay a visit to this friendly fairy
and soon feel better.

III

FRIENDS TO THE BEES

Bees love to visit flowers and fairies in the garden, and they are especially pleased to visit SNAPDRAGON. They dive straight into his blossoms until their bodies are hidden and then sip at the nectar inside. When the bees have drunk as much as they can, they reverse out of the flower backward! Snapdragon himself looks upon all this with fondness, and if he sees a bee that's shy he hails him with a song:

Snapdragon's name is only a game—
It isn't as fierce as it sounds;
The Snapdragon Elf is pleased as Punch
When Bumble comes on his rounds!

All Flower Fairies are good friends
with the honeybees. They help by
guiding them to their fullest blooms
and standing protectively beside
them as the buzzing insects collect the
pollen. In return, the bees provide a
regular supply of delicious honey for
all the fairies to enjoy.

FRIENDSHIP FUN

One of the best things about having a friend is always having someone to play with. Flower Fairies are great playmates and very good at putting their heads together to think of new games and activities.

If you would like to have fun just like a Flower Fairy, why not try some of their ideas?

FAIRY SPOTTERS

When you and your friends go out for the day, see who can spot and identify the most trees and flowers. Award a point for each one spotted, and an extra five points for spotting and naming an unusual or rare flower. Ten points to anyone who spots a Flower Fairy!

Fairy Art

Make gorgeous cards
and collages with your
friends, using pressed flowers
like the ones described on pages
98–9. You can also try making your
own decorated bookmarks
or gift tags.

Daisy Crown

Make a hole in the stem of
a daisy, then thread another
stem through it. Repeat until
you have a chain long enough
to make a crown like the one
DAISY is wearing. Try making
necklaces and bracelets too.

Fairy Wishes

Do you have a special wish? Write it down on a
piece of paper and sign it with your fairy name
(see pages 194–5 for how to work out your fairy
name). Fold it in half, kiss the paper, close your
eyes, and think of the Flower Fairy you love the
most. Now hide the paper somewhere, and your
chosen fairy will try her best to make your
wish come true!

THE FRIENDSHIP CODE

To be a true friend of
the Flower Fairies you must:

❀ Be kind, loving, and helpful.

❀ Take care of the animals
and plants around you.

❀ Have lots of fun and love to laugh.

❀ Believe in the Flower Fairies!

Most fairies live in large communities among the flowers and trees, and they look upon the members of their particular group as their own family. They cook together, hold family parties and celebrations, and generally look after one another.

Within each fairy family there are usually several fairy children of different ages. All of them need to be cared for, fed, and kept out of trouble or danger. This job falls to the older fairies, who act as their parents. And just like human parents, they need to be strict sometimes!

Fairy Babies

Just like humans, Flower Fairies need
to be cared for when they are young.

The babies crawl and clamber around
their plants, falling off and getting into
mischief. So the older Flower Fairies look
after the little ones.

APPLE BLOSSOM clings on tightly
to her sister, high up in the treetops!

GUELDER ROSE shows her little
sister how to look after their flowers.

SILVER BIRCH
and SYCAMORE
teach the babies how
to swing around their
plants safely.

Every single older
Flower Fairy has the job of
teaching the young ones how
to care for their plant.

Most of the time, Flower Fairy
babies just play! PANSY teaches them
how to dance.

Parties with Poppy

POPPY is one of the oldest fairies and enjoys arranging parties and other treats for the fairy children. In the summer, when her flowers are in full bloom, Poppy invites all the baby fairies over to her plant. She sits them all inside one of the silky blossoms and offers them bowls of poppy seeds, which are just like popcorn for fairies!

Poppy petals are a beautiful deep red
and as fine as tissue paper. They make
wonderful lanterns for parties. When
moonlight filters through the delicate
flowers, everything is bathed in a magical
light, tinged with the palest pink.

Dressing Up with Sweet Pea

All the fairy babies in the garden love SWEET PEA, especially the girls. Sweet Pea has a fabulous collection of outfits that she likes to dress up the babies in, just as if they were dolls! Sweet Pea has a little sister, whom she spoils with all of her best dressing-up clothes. When little Sweet Pea grows up, she will be the most fashionable fairy around!

A delicate lacy dress to impress the Fairy Queen.

Flouncy collars and sleeves are just the thing.

Velvety blue petals feel soft and cozy.

Does it suit you, Baby?
Yes, I really think
Nothing's more becoming
Than this pretty pink!

Dainty blossoms adorn a petal skirt.

Petal petticoats are perfect for fairy balls.

WHITE BINDWEED'S SONG

O long long stems that twine!
O buds, so neatly furled!
O great white bells of mine,
(None purer in the world)
Each lasting but one day!
O leafy garlands, hung
In wreaths beside the way—
Well may your praise be sung!

FAIRY FASHION

F

LOWER FAIRIES have very special clothes. All the fairies wear outfits made from the leaves and petals of their own plant or flower, which makes it easy for them to hide.

White Bindweed's bonnet is made from her leaves.

Gaillardia wears shorts and boots made from his leaves.

Cornflower wears a crown of blue flowers.

126

Fumitory's skirts are the colors of her plant.

Look at Marigold's necklace of golden petals.

Sloe has spots on her dress just like her berries.

Fuchsia's dress looks exactly like her bell-shaped flowers.

Fairy Disguises

The fairies are proud of their clever disguises and try to think of original ideas for garments and accessories. The materials they use for their dresses, skirts, stockings, and shorts are carefully selected for their color and freshness. Seedpods, petals, buds, and leaves are transformed into hats, bonnets, shoes, and bags. Pretty headbands and necklaces are threaded out of dried seeds and grass. And because all fairies design their own clothes for TANSY to sew, no two outfits are ever the same!

Bugle's bonnet is a bugle blossom.

Bugle's shoes are made from his bronzy leaves.

Wayfaring Tree's leaves are cleverly stitched together to make her hat.

See how Wayfaring Tree's sandals match her handbag!

129

Hats and All That

It's very important that a fairy's hat fits perfectly (because of all the flying!), and although an adult fairy's head will always be between the size of a hawthorn berry and an acorn, some fairies just won't sit still long enough for SWEET PEA to measure them!

Many fairies make pretty caps or bonnets from their flowers, but SWEET CHESTNUT has a spiky helmet made from the chestnut's case, and the heart of a flower makes a sparkling golden crown for KINGCUP.

You will need:

Tape measure

Cardboard

Scissors

Stapler

Green crepe paper

Tissue paper:
4 purple, 2 blue

Pencil

Saucer

Small cup
2 inches across

Glue
and brush

CORNFLOWER'S CROWN

This wonderful crown of blooms completes Cornflower's outfit. Here's how you can make one too.

1. Measure around the top of your head. Cut out a strip of card 1 inch longer than your head and 1.5 inches wide, then staple the ends together.

Cornflower's craft tip

You can make this crown in other pretty colors too, such as pale pink or lilac.

2. Cut a strip of crepe paper, 40 inches long and 2.5 inches wide. Glue one end inside the crown, then wind around the crown. Glue the loose end.

3. Lay the four sheets of purple tissue paper on top of each other. Draw around the rim of the saucer ten times. Cut out the circles.

4. Lay the two sheets of blue tissue paper on top of each other and draw around the rim of the cup ten times. Cut out the circles.

5. For each flower, place two blue circles on top of four purple circles. Fold in half. Fold over twice more.

6. Carefully make four cuts from the edge of the paper toward the center, then snip the edges, as shown.

7. Gently unfold the circles, separate them, and put a dab of glue in the center of each layer.

8. Pinch the bottom part of the flower and glue on to your headband. Repeat for each flower.

In the Bag

What do you think Flower Fairies might need to carry with them? If you were to peek inside a fairy's private purse, you might find:

My Diary

A little book for fairy notes and dreams

Fairy dust

Fairy coins

Fairy hair brush

Summer Fairy Ball

An invitation to the Summer Fairy Ball!

Tip Tap Toe

If you had a little look inside a Flower Fairy's wardrobe, you might find . . .

Summer sandals

Light and airy shoes for a hot summer

Dancing slippers

These would make any fairy light on her toes.

Special occasions

Flashy and dandy!

Winter boots

Boots keep tiny tootsies snug.

Pretty fairy footwear can finish off an outfit perfectly, and there are so many different styles to choose from.

Wings to Flutter By

When Flower Fairies are first born, their wings are as delicate as cobwebs, but soon they become strong and colorful. Like snowflakes, each fairy's wings are different from the next, but all are sprinkled with magic. Early in the morning, wings glisten with dew, and the rising sun makes them reflect rainbow colors.

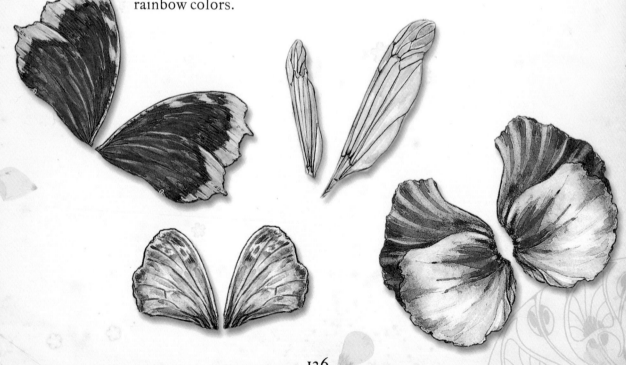

DAINTY PRETTY THINGS

Makeup

For special occasions, a fairy might add some color to her cheeks and lips using squashed berries.

Jewelery

Fairy jewels are made by stringing together buds, petals, and berries.

Every fairy has a natural scent from the flowers she looks after, but all agree that these flowers make the best perfume:

Almond Blossom   Lavender   Rose   Bluebell   Sweet Pea

You will need:

Flour and salt

Tablespoon

Bowl

Measuring cup

Baking tray

Cookie cutter

Metal skewer

Acrylic paint

Paintbrush

Glue

Narrow ribbon

Darning needle

Marigold's Fairy Charms

Marigold loves to design pretty charms for her friends. They are fun to make and sure to bring good luck!

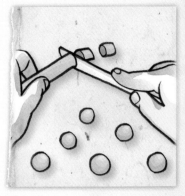

1. Using the recipe on the opposite page, make up the salt dough. Cut flower shapes in rolled-out dough with a cookie cutter.

2. To make beads, roll the dough into a thin tube between your hands, then cut into 1/4 x 1/4 inch squares. Roll into balls with your fingers.

3. Ask an adult to push the beads on to a skewer, and make a hole in each flower shape using a skewer.

4. Ask an adult to help you bake the salt dough in the oven (see recipe for instructions) then leave to cool.

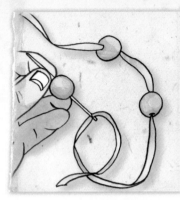

5. Paint the charms with acrylic paint. When dry, add a coat of glue mixed with water to make them dazzle.

6. Thread a darning needle with ribbon, and push through the holes in the jewelery. Now your charms are ready to wear!

If you're making beads, it's much easier to paint them while they are still on the metal skewer.

Salt Dough Recipe

2 cups of flour
1 cup of salt
1 cup lukewarm water

Mix the flour and salt together, then slowly add the water until it binds together to form a dough. Knead the dough until it is smooth, then leave it for half an hour before use.

Bake the finished models at 265 °F until they are golden brown and sound hollow when tapped. Make sure you wear oven gloves, and ask an adult to help you. Small beads will take around 45 minutes. A larger pendant shape will take up to an hour and a half.

CRAB-APPLE FAIRY'S SONG

Crab-apples, Crab-apples,
   out in the wood,
Little and bitter,
   yet little and good!
The apples in orchards,
   so rosy and fine,
Are children of wild
   little apples like mine.
The branches are laden,
   and droop to the ground;
The fairy-fruit falls
   in a circle around.

FAIRY
FOOD

FAIRY DINING ROOMS are warm and welcoming, with plenty of room for guests. Plants and mushrooms are used for furniture, and tables are set with bowls and cups made from empty acorn cups, seedpods, and halves of nutshells. The tree fairies collect them for their friends, and because they work so hard, there is a never-ending supply of fairy "crockery."

An upturned Canterbury bell makes an excellent dining table.

Sturdy mushrooms make perfect stools for fairies.

Flower Fairies eat nuts and
berries. With honey from the bees
and fruit from the trees, the fairies
make fragrant wines, sweet jams and
delicious fairy jellies.

Hazel-Nut gathers in her harvest.

Crab-Apple catches her fruits
to make scrumptious jelly.

Mallow's seeds make
the finest fairy cheeses.

143

Picnics and Tea Parties

Because fairies are outdoor creatures, most of their meals are eaten in the open air, and if the weather is good there is nothing they like better than a picnic with lots of friends. Every fairy brings a basket of delicious treats to share. For this picnic, BLACKBERRY has brought her juiciest berries, ELDER has made delicious elderflower cordial, and SWEET CHESTNUT is throwing down his tastiest nuts. There is usually more than enough to eat and drink, so any leftovers are given to the squirrels and other animals that live nearby.

If the fairies want to make more of an occasion out of their meal, they might have a proper tea party. Tea parties are very popular, as all fairies love eating fairy cakes and drinking jasmine tea. If a fairy decides to host a tea party, she will send proper invitations to her guests. Fairies have excellent manners in this respect and they would never forget to reply to an invitation or to say "Thank you" after a party.

DEAR YOU . . . LOVE ME!

Flower Fairies love parties, and making invitations is a fun part of preparing for the special occasion. Try making these beautiful "Fairy Wing" invitations.

Supplies to gather:

White paper
Green fabric (felt or cotton)
Beads or sequins
Pressed flowers
Markers or
colored pencils
Scissors (ask an adult)
Glue

1. Take a piece of white paper and fold it in half.

2. Draw a wing, like half a butterfly, with the wing sprouting out of the folded edge. Use the picture opposite to help you.

3. Cut around the edge of the wing. When you open it out, you should have a butterfly shape.

4. To make wings like those of the Poplar Fairy, cut out some green fabric (using your card as a template) and stick onto back of the paper.

5. Glue some beads or sparkly sequins on the front of the card, and use a marker or colored pencil to draw on some delicate markings. When everything is dry, you're ready to write your card!

Dear
[insert fairy's name]

Please come to my

Flower Fairies party!

At . . . .

Date . . . . . .

Time . . . .

Home-made cards are the finest, all fairies agree,
Add glitter, some color and an RSVP!

Remember to bring your
very best smile!

With love from,
[insert your name],

R.S.V.P.

Fairy Craft Tip
No two fairies have the
same wings, so don't worry
if your invitations are
not identical!

Sipping and Nibbling

Fairies love to host fabulous fairy feasts. Their kitchens and pantries are always filled with yummy ripe fruits and tasty crunchy nuts. In the summertime, for example, the little **STRAWBERRY FAIRY** is very busy harvesting all his fruit. It is delicious to eat on its own, but were you to visit Strawberry in the summer, he might offer you some of his special fairy nectar.

Strawberry's Secret Fairy Nectar

Blend together a handful of strawberries with a glass of orange juice and a tablespoon each of yogurt and honey. Be sure to ask a grown-up fairy to help you use the blender.

Fairy Cookbook

148

STRAWBERRY'S PANTRY

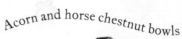

Dishes and bowls

Acorn and horse chestnut bowls

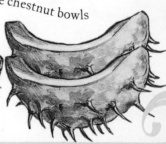

Fruit and nuts

Cutlery

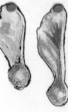

Sycamore wings are used as serving spoons.

Fairy nectar

The fairies search the gardens and meadows for cups and glasses.

At the end of every fabulous feast, there's lots of cleaning up to do!

Just what you need for scrubbing out that pan!

A hazel catkin is used as a scrub brush.

Cooking a Feast

There are Flower Fairy recipes for every season. But always make sure you have an adult helper when you're cutting or cooking.

Kitchen Rules!
❀ Always ask permission before you start to cook.
❀ Ask an adult to help you.
❀ Wash your hands!
❀ Clean up as you go along.

Fluttery Fruit Cups

To serve 4 fairies:
2 ripe peaches (or nectarines)
A selection of extra fruit
Small pot of crème fraîche
Vanilla wafers

1. Wash the fruit. Carefully cut the peaches in half, remove the pits, and scoop the flesh out of each peach half, leaving a solid rim. Cut the scooped-out flesh into little chunks.

2. Chop the other fruit into similar-sized chunks.

3. Mix all the fruit together, then fill the peach halves.

4. Top with a spoonful of crème fraîche. Stick two vanilla wafers in each peach half to look like fairy wings.

If there is any cake left, you can keep it in the fridge for a few days, but don't freeze it again.

Special Strawberry Treat Cake

To serve 10 fairies:
12 strawberries
Small box of graham crackers
4 small cartons of sour cream
Powdered sugar
A little butter

1. Preheat the oven to 300°F.

2. Rub a little butter over a medium-sized cake tin that has a removable base.

3. Empty the crackers into a clean plastic bag and crush them with a rolling pin. Pour the crumbs into the cake tin and press down with a fork.

4. Pour the sour cream into a big bowl. Wash out one of the cartons, dry it, then fill it with powdered sugar and pour into the sour cream.

5. Wash, dry, and halve the strawberries. Squash three with a fork. Add the whole and squashed strawberries to the mixture. Stir gently. Pour the mixture over the cracker base.

6. Put the cake in the oven for about half an hour. It should wobble slightly when it is cooked.

7. Take out of the oven, leave until completely cold, and then freeze overnight. Remove the cake four hours before you need to slice and eat it. Remove from the tin, but leave on the base to serve. Decorate with extra strawberries!

You will need:

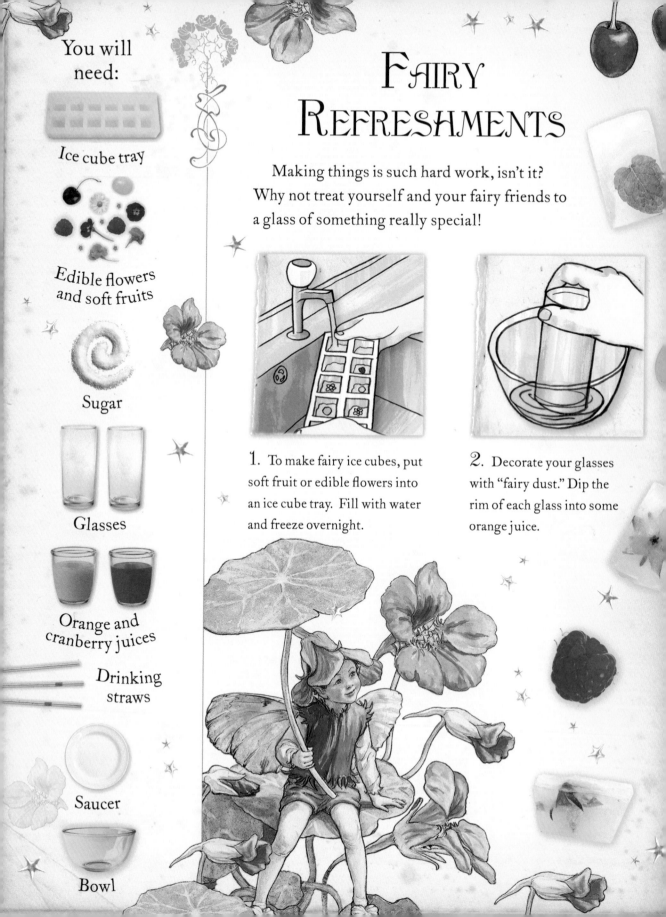

Ice cube tray

Edible flowers and soft fruits

Sugar

Glasses

Orange and cranberry juices

Drinking straws

Saucer

Bowl

FAIRY REFRESHMENTS

Making things is such hard work, isn't it? Why not treat yourself and your fairy friends to a glass of something really special!

1. To make fairy ice cubes, put soft fruit or edible flowers into an ice cube tray. Fill with water and freeze overnight.

2. Decorate your glasses with "fairy dust." Dip the rim of each glass into some orange juice.

3. Dip the glass into a saucer of sugar. This gives a frosted, glittery "fairy dust" effect!

4. Add ice cubes and chopped fruit to the glass. Fill halfway with some fresh orange juice.

5. Carefully fill the rest of your glass with delicious cranberry juice.

6. Use your favorite fruits to decorate. Try different combinations of juices and fruit!

Nasturtium's craft tips

❀ Only use the following flowers for your ice cubes:
Rose petals
Violet petals
Chamomile flowers
Nasturtiums
Mint

THE FAIRY MARKET

As dusk falls in the woods, hundreds of fairies are beginning to gather for one of their favorite events—the Fairy Market. This is where fairies go to buy, sell, and barter their wares. A fairy can find anything he or she might want or need here, and there is plenty of fairy food to be had, with many stalls selling hot chestnuts, fruits, berries, cakes, and refreshing juices. Other things to buy are tiny fairy shoes, beautiful jewelery, trinkets, crockery, and musical instruments.

The market is always held at night because this is the safest time for the fairies to meet, away from the eyes and ears of sleeping humans. There is a happy, bustling atmosphere as hundreds of fairies wander around, their baskets laden with goods. Some fairies are chatting, others are munching on delicious snacks, while others are singing and dancing. All the fairies make the most of this big, friendly gathering.

KINGCUP FAIRY'S SONG

Golden King of marsh and swamp,
Reigning in your springtime pomp,
Hear the little elves you've found
Trespassing on royal ground:—

'Please, your Kingship, we were told
Of your shining cups of gold;
So we came here, just to see—
Not to rob your Majesty!'
Golden Kingcup, well I know
You will smile and let them go!
Yet let human folk beware
How they thieve and trespass there:

Kingcup-laden, they may lose
In the swamp their boots and shoes!

The Fairy King and Queen

THE PEACEFUL MARSH is home to the King and Queen of the Flower Fairies, KINGCUP and QUEEN OF THE MEADOW. The royal couple rule all of Flower Fairyland and are kind, generous and wise, always ready to listen to their fairies, and to offer advice or help. They often leave the marsh to visit their fairy subjects and the Queen will ride upon a swallow on these occasions.

The Queen of the Meadow wears no crown upon her soft golden hair. Instead she wears a necklace of large green pearls to complement her ivory silken gown. All the creatures of the marshlands are in her service, from minnows and water beetles to kingfishers and dragonflies.

Elegant Kingcup glows like a ray of sunshine with
his shimmering yellow tunic and glossy golden locks.
He wears a crown of Kingcup stamens, an amber
necklace and a flowing leafy cloak.

The BUTTERCUP Fairy is princess of the royal
kingdom and her many flowers are the royal family's gift to
anyone who wanders in the marsh and meadows and wishes to
pick them. Outgoing and friendly, Buttercup fills the marshes
and fields with her yellow flowers, which she polishes until
they shine like gold. Their sunny colour gives pleasure to all
her fairy friends and to human children too.

ZINNIA FAIRY'S SONG

Z for Zinnias, pink or red;
See them in the flower-bed,
Copper, orange, all aglow,
Making such a stately show.

SECRET STORIES

ZINNIA'S MAGICAL ADVENTURE

Chapter One
Babysitting

"YES, YOUR MAJESTY, I AGREE. Daisy does make quite the best fairy nectar in the garden," Zinnia said, lifting her bluebell cup and pretending to take a dainty sip. Daisy giggled as she got to her feet, gathering the petals of her skirt in either hand. "Show me how you curtsy again," she said, putting out a leg in front of her and wobbling as she tried to bob down without losing her balance.

"Watch out!" Double Daisy shouted. "Or you'll land in the crab-apple jelly—and imagine what the Queen of the Meadow would think of that!"

The two young Flower Fairies burst out laughing. Zinnia smiled to herself. Her little cousins were very sweet and she loved spending time with them, but it had been a long morning since Daisy had come up with the idea of a make-believe royal tea party. Zinnia had made special daisy-chain garlands for each of them and patiently tried to teach them how they should bow and curtsy in front of a queen. Double Daisy would lean so far forward that the red petals from his bonnet kept flopping in his eyes, causing him to topple over, and he and his sister to fall down laughing. And, of course, no matter how many times he did it, the funnier the two of them found it.

It had been very funny at first and Zinnia had been happy to have imaginary conversations with their regal guest, but now she was getting a bit bored of the game and longed to stretch her legs.

She couldn't help
wondering what Beechnut
and Hazel-Nut were up
to. These adventurous
fairies were always
bursting with energy
and up for a game of
tag. The trouble was
that they lived in the
lane outside the garden
boundaries. And Daisy and
Double Daisy were too little to stray far
from their flowers and too young to be left on their own.

Now they were concentrating hard on carrying bark plates piled high with
imaginary food, supposedly presenting them to their guest. They were also
arguing about whether the Queen of the Meadow would have arrived in a
chariot pulled by dragonflies or if she would have flown in from the marshes
on the back of a bird.

Zinnia sighed. It had been ages since she had been out of the garden,
and it suddenly struck her that she must have been
missing out on all sorts of excitement.
Beechnut and Hazel-Nut got to
see everything from their
vantage point in the
trees and they were
always full of interesting
stories—for one thing, lots of
different humans used the lane to go
about their daily business. Zinnia often
spent time imagining what it would be like
to live somewhere less predictable than the garden.

"You're daydreaming again!" a voice from above interrupted her thoughts.

Zinnia looked up. A Flower Fairy with rosy cheeks and pretty pink wings was sitting on the bough of the apple tree, swinging her legs.

"Apple Blossom!"

Zinnia was very pleased to see her friend. She was always cheerful and never got tired of playing with the younger Flower Fairies.

"I was just thinking it might be nice to see what's going on in the lane this afternoon . . ." Zinnia paused. She suddenly had an idea. "Um . . . but of course I'm looking after my cousins," she went on, "and I would ask Sweet Pea, but she's busy teaching the baby fairies to climb—"

"I'd love to look after Daisy and Double Daisy," Apple Blossom interrupted. "Off you go, and have an adventure!" She began nimbly swinging from branch to branch until she was perched on the tip of the one nearest to the ground.

"Oh, you're wonderful!" Zinnia beamed as Apple Blossom flew down and landed on the grass.

The Tree Fairy gathered up Daisy in an enormous hug and then swung Double Daisy round and round by his arms.

"What are you up to, my lovelies?"

"We're having tea with the Queen of the Meadow, of course," the two Daisies chorused.

"Well, good afternoon, Your Highness, what an honor," Apple Blossom said, winking at Zinnia and curtsying very low to the space between the two young Flower Fairies.

Zinnia waved good-bye and blew a kiss to her cousins. They would have a great time with Apple Blossom, and she'd be back long before their bedtime. As she headed for the wall at the bottom of the garden, there was a definite spring to her step, and she felt a sudden surge of excitement. She had the whole afternoon to herself, and who knew what lay ahead of her?

Chapter Two
High Up!

"Horse Chestnut! Where are you?" Zinnia called, parting the large green leaves of his tree to peer up among the higher branches. She had made light work of the garden wall, which was old stone and had plenty of footholds, and, after a quick look up and down the lane to check it was safe, she had flown straight for her friend's tree.

"Horse Chestnut, are you there?"

Zinnia ran lightly along the length of the branch until she was right inside the canopy of leaves, where she leaned against the trunk of the tree to catch her breath. She tucked a loose strand of hair behind her ear and straightened the daisy garland on her head, expecting Horse Chestnut's mischievous face to appear at any moment.

Mind you, she thought, *it would be more like him to come whizzing out of nowhere and surprise me!*

Horse Chestnut always dressed entirely in green and brown, including his green spiky helmet, so he was quite difficult to spot and was an expert at sudden appearances.

"Today I will be ready for him," Zinnia said resolutely, thinking aloud. She listened intently for any sign of movement but could only hear the distant song of a blackbird and the leaves of the tree stirring gently in the breeze.

After a few moments without any sign of Horse Chestnut, Zinnia began to relax. She watched a field mouse dart across the dusty lane and scurry into a hedgerow, and she wondered if Horse Chestnut had gone to visit Beechnut. She would go and look for both of them in a minute, she decided, but for now she was enjoying her view of the world from above. Being high up made her aware that she was out in a much larger open space than usual, and compared to the garden, with its familiar beds and borders, it seemed to brim with possibilities.

At that moment, Zinnia's thoughts were interrupted by the sound of excited chatter followed by a loud laugh. It seemed to be coming from farther up the lane. And if she wasn't mistaken, it was the sound of *human* children heading toward her!

Taking care to be as quiet as she could, Zinnia crept along the branch to get a better view. Luckily there was a particularly large horse chestnut leaf for her to hide behind, and, flattening her wings against her back, she made sure that none of the bright pink petals of her skirt were poking out.

You see, Flower Fairies can see humans, and they know all about them. They are even allowed to help humans, but on no account are they ever to let humans catch sight of them. When Zinnia had officially been given her flower and become a proper Flower Fairy, wise Wild Rose had explained to her that generally humans were very friendly. However, they were also curious beings —especially children—and if they knew that there really were fairies living in their world and even in their own gardens, they would never leave them alone, and it would be impossible for the Flower Fairy Garden to continue its peaceful existence.

Zinnia took a deep breath and bravely popped her head out from behind the leaf. She had seen the humans that lived in the house at the top of the garden on numerous occasions, but the insects feel the vibrations in the grass first and would always give the fairies ample warning. This time Zinnia was unprepared and she was alone.

The children were nearly below the tree now. A boy and a girl with dark hair and very similar features were hurrying along at quite a pace, and a smaller girl with flushed red cheeks was struggling to keep up with them.

"Come on, Emily, you're such a slowpoke!" the boy called to her.

"Shut up, Tom," she replied, puffing. "If it wasn't for me you'd still be complaining about how boring playing in the garden is."

"And she was the last one to climb over the gate," his twin sister reminded him.

"Anyway, because it was Emily's idea to explore the marsh she should lead the way."

"Who made you expedition organizer, Charlotte?" Tom said, but Zinnia could see that he had a grin on his face, and he'd slowed down so that his younger sister could catch up.

"Will there be quicksand? Who do you think we'll meet on the marsh? Do wild animals live there?" Emily chirped away, too busy asking questions to wait for the answers.

Zinnia watched them disappearing down the lane, not moving a muscle for several moments. The Flower Fairy wasn't fixed to the spot because she was afraid they'd catch sight of her—they had been so absorbed in their conversation that they hadn't even looked up once—but because she'd had a brainstorm. She'd never been to the marsh, and she'd certainly never met any of the Wild Flower Fairies that lived there. Their very name suggested that they must be far more exotic than any of the fairies Zinnia knew. That was it! Forget playing tag in the lane—she was off for a real adventure.

"Show me the way!" she called boldly after the retreating figures, knowing that her voice was too tiny for them to hear at a distance. With that, she took a joyous leap into the air and beat her wings as fast as she could in order to follow the children.

Chapter Three
Time to Explore

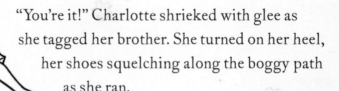

"You're it!" Charlotte shrieked with glee as she tagged her brother. She turned on her heel, her shoes squelching along the boggy path as she ran.

"Mom's going to kill us!" Emily giggled as she dived into the long rush-grass, just managing to escape Tom's grasp.

The marsh was like nowhere Zinnia had ever been before.

The children had climbed over a stile that led directly from the lane on to the marsh, and she had done her best to keep up with them as they splashed along the waterlogged path that cut across it. They whooped and called to one another, flitting in and out of the tall grasses that seemed more like a forest to the Flower Fairy than the short, spiky grass that neatly bordered the flower bed where she lived.

When finally the children had taken a break from their game to catch their breath, Zinnia landed on a grass with dense and cottony heads. It provided her with a comfortable resting place. The marshland seemed to stretch as far as she could see in every direction—a sea of grass that met the horizon, the muted green unbroken by any of the bright flowers or blossom trees that she was accustomed to.

In comparison, the fuchsia pink of her skirt looked even more dazzling than usual, and so she had to be doubly careful not to let the children spot her. At first, Zinnia had flown behind them at a safe distance, but soon she became bolder, and it wasn't long before she was so close that if they'd turned their heads she wouldn't have more than a split second to hide.

And then it became a game of dare—weaving in and out of the grasses after the children, or darting on to the path and flying right behind them before plunging back amidst the stalks at the last moment.

Phew! she thought to herself as she sank back into the fluffy cushions. *Apple Blossom and the Daisies will never believe how far I've flown today.* She smiled to herself, imagining their surprise.

Garden Flower Fairies don't fly long distances—they walk as much as they can and tend to take to the air to get up into the trees or just for fun. If they have farther to go they hitch a lift with a friendly bird or dragonfly. Zinnia was just picturing her friends' faces as she told them all about the children and following them to the marsh, when a flash of purple caught her eye. She felt a rush of adrenaline. Could it be one of the Wild Flower Fairies that she'd come to meet? Tingling with anticipation, she launched herself into the air to find out.

When she landed she headed in the direction she thought the fairy had taken. And sure enough—just beyond the path, behind a clump of rush-grass—sat not just one Flower Fairy, but three!

The fairy that Zinnia had seen sat with her knees pulled up to her chin, a torn green smock all but covering her purple-petal dress, and her long brown hair pulled back in two messy plaits. She had beautiful purple-and-white wings, but Zinnia was shocked to see how dusty they looked—she had never come across a Flower Fairy that seemed to care less about her appearance! Cross-legged in front of her were two boy fairies—both with pointed ears, plain white wings, and, Zinnia noticed, clothes the color of the surrounding grasses. In fact, one of them had tufty blond hair like the flower head that she'd sat on, and the other wore a grass girdle around his tunic that was hemmed with small brown seeds.

"Er, hello," she ventured, feeling quite nervous as she stepped out into the clearing.

"Wow, look at you!" the female Flower Fairy burst out, jumping to her feet. "I've never seen such magnificent wings."

"They're the same as the painted lady butterflies," Zinnia said timidly. "And my skirt is from my flower—Zinnia," she added, quite taken aback by the confident fairy who was walking slowly around her, openly admiring her clothes.

"I'm Mallow, but most people call me Rags-and-Tatters on account of the state of me!" Mallow laughed warmly, and Zinnia couldn't help but like her immediately.

"And I'm Cotton-Grass, and this is my brother Rush-Grass," the blond boy fairy said, pointing to his companion, whose face broke into a broad grin.

"Come and join us—we've been spying on some newcomers," said Mallow, cocking her head in the direction of the sound of the children's chatter. She sat down and patted the ground next to her. "And you're certainly not from around here, looking as neat as a new pin!"

"I'm from the garden," Zinnia explained. "Quite a long way from here, actually," she went on, no longer feeling shy.

"Oh, the garden," Rush-Grass said. "Heard all about it, but never been myself."

"I've seen it once." Mallow nodded wisely. "Peeked over the wall on my travels. I sell my seeds as fairy cheeses at the market. Fairy housewives and elves can't get enough of them!" she explained, picking up from beside her what looked to Zinnia like a miniature pumpkin.

"That garden's very cozy-looking," said Cotton-Grass.

"Sounds a bit tame, if you ask me," Rush-Grass piped up, but not unkindly.

Zinnia wasn't sure if she liked her home being called cozy or tame. It was very ordered, and life was comfortable there, but she didn't want the marsh dwellers to think she was boring.

"Oh, but there's always plenty going on. And um, I don't really spend much time there—I'm always off exploring," she boasted uncertainly.

"Well, you should come and see the sights with us. Never a dull moment on the marsh. Every day's an adventure!" Cotton-Grass said enthusiastically. "And the best part is that we never know where we'll be at nightfall."

"What do you mean?" Zinnia asked, enthralled.

"Sleep where we end up—make do with whatever pillow we can find, of course!" Rush-Grass exclaimed, jumping to his feet and stretching his arms out wide.

"You should try it. Nothing beats sleeping out—with nothing between you and the stars. How about tonight?" Cotton-Grass offered.

Zinnia gulped. The thought of darkness drawing in without the comfort of her familiar flower or a moss blanket to pull over her wasn't very appealing—even if it was an adventure . . . But on the other hand, she couldn't let her new friends think she was any less courageous than them. No—she would show them what a Garden Flower Fairy was made of!

Chapter Four
New Friends

Just then there was a low whistle from a nearby clump of grass.

"Hey, Cotton, Rush—come here. I think you're needed," whispered Mallow, who had wandered off to keep an eye on the children.

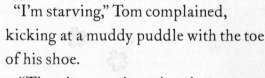

Zinnia had been vaguely aware of the absence of laughter and the tone of the children's voices changing. And now, as she peeked over Mallow's shoulder, it was obvious that they were no longer enjoying themselves.

They were quite a different sight from the three children who had been in high spirits earlier that afternoon. Aside from the messy state of their clothes, they looked tired and decidedly miserable.

"I'm starving," Tom complained, kicking at a muddy puddle with the toe of his shoe.

"There's no use in saying that over and over again," said Charlotte. "You know we've missed snack time and we'll be lucky if Mom doesn't send us to bed without anything to eat."

"And we still haven't found my shoe," Emily wailed. She was in particularly bad shape—her plump little legs and feet were caked in mud, and her skirt was covered in grass stains. Zinnia thought she looked quite comical, and it reminded her of her Daisy cousins, which in turn made her feel quite homesick.

"Seeing as you don't even know when it came off, we're never going to find it," Tom said grumpily. "And I don't know about you, but I have no idea what direction we came from."

Charlotte, who was frantically searching through the grass, looked up. "We just need to find the path, and then even if we go in the wrong direction at least we'll know the other way will take us back to the lane," she said, looking less sure than she sounded.

"That's our job," Rush-Grass whispered to Zinnia. "We help whoever's got lost on the marsh to find their way home."

"How do you do that without them seeing you though?" Zinnia asked.

"A little bit of fairy dust and a bit more speed," chortled Cotton-Grass, who was unfolding a large dock leaf that he had been carrying as a knapsack.

"People generally follow bright lights, even if it isn't dark—it makes them feel hopeful." Rush-Grass beamed at Zinnia. "So we just catch their eye with some fairy dust, make some noise, and then fly to the path as fast as we can." He took a handful of the fine powder.

"Perhaps you should go back with them," Mallow suggested. "It's time that I got myself ready for market tomorrow, so I'd better be off."

Zinnia was about to gratefully agree when she remembered their conversation about the garden and how she'd boasted about being adventurous. Although she wasn't sure she knew her way home, she felt confident that if she flew above the grass she'd get her bearings quickly enough. "Oh, don't worry about me," she said cheerily. "I've still got some exploring to do."

"Travel well, then," Cotton said, opening his wings.

"Farewell, ladies," said his brother. As he took off, he blew the fairy dust into the air. "Light up!" he commanded.

Zinnia watched the tiny particles glow to life and dance away on the breeze. "Good-bye!" she called as the Grass Fairies followed.

"Well," said Mallow, turning to the Garden Fairy and taking her hands, "it's been lovely to meet you, and I hope it's not the last time." She turned to go and then, as an afterthought, held out a fat mallow seed.

Zinnia took it gratefully and waved as her friend disappeared through the tall grass. "Maybe see you later?" she called after her, as it suddenly struck her that she was completely alone again.

"I'll eat the cheese and then I'll be on my way," Zinnia said, thinking aloud into the silence. It wasn't until she sat down that she realized how tired she was—all the excitement had kept her exhaustion at bay, but now her wings positively ached. "If only I'd brought some fairy dust with me."

Flower Fairies cannot cast spells as such, but ground-up pollen from each of their flowers gives them a little magic of their own. Walking all the way home seemed like an impossible task to Zinnia, but if she had some of her fairy dust she could have summoned the butterflies to accompany her.

Perhaps I am going to have to sleep here tonight, she thought as she took a bite of the cheese. The mallow seed was delicious and instantly comforting and somehow helped her forget about her butterfly friends: some of Mallow's magic. Zinnia smiled as her spirits lifted further, and she reminded herself that plenty of Wild Flower Fairies slept out on the marsh, so it couldn't be that frightening.

She was just thinking that Cotton-Grass and Rush-Grass might be back before too long when she was startled by a rustling in the grass behind her. She looked around, expecting to see an insect or a bird, but there was no one.

There it was again—more rustling, but this time to the left of her, and it was followed by a stifled giggle.

"Rush? Cotton? Is that you?"

But there was no answer, just more rustling.

"Mallow?" Zinnia called optimistically, hoping that her friend had finished her work quickly and come back to find her.

The Garden Fairy got to her feet and shivered. The heat had gone out of the afternoon sun, and for the first time she noticed how much colder it was without the shelter of the garden wall.

I may as well start heading home, she thought. *Even if I don't find the path, at least moving will warm me up.*

Hearing another giggle, Zinnia hurried to pick up the remainder of the mallow seed. But she was too late—the grasses parted and two creatures dressed entirely in dark green rushed out at her.

"Fairy cheese and a pretty little fairy to go with it!" said one gleefully, and the other snatched the seed from her hands, causing her to lose her balance.

Zinnia looked up at the sly eyes staring back at her; then she looked at the long, pointed ears and the hoods covering messy hair. And finally she noticed not only the lack of shoes but, more importantly, the pointed wings on the back of the creatures.

"You're elves!" Zinnia gasped, and before she could stop herself, she burst into tears.

CHAPTER FIVE
NAUGHTY ELVES

"Crybaby! Crybaby!" chanted the elves, dancing round Zinnia in delight.

At first they had been stunned into silence by the Garden Fairy's outburst, but now that she had dried her eyes and was looking cross rather than sad, they had set about poking fun at her.

After shedding a few tears, Zinnia felt a lot better, and now the elves were infuriating her. Their energy seemed to be limitless, and no matter how many times she tried to dodge past one of them, the other would be there, barring her way. "Give me back my cheese and let me go!" she exclaimed, trying to grab the mallow seed from the nearest elf as he blocked her path.

But he threw it over her head to his companion, giggling almost uncontrollably.

"Can't give you the cheese—that's ours for the eating," said the other elf, taking an enormous bite and all but finishing it off. "But you're free to go whenever you want. Isn't she?" He winked at his friend and threw him back the last of the mallow seed.

"Although that's not to say we won't follow you, pretty one," mocked his mate, cramming what was left into his mouth.

"Elves—you're trespassing!" boomed a voice that stopped all three of them in their tracks. The next moment into the clearing walked the most resplendent Flower Fairy Zinnia had ever seen. He was older than her with a distinguished air about him, but he had a youthful, handsome face. Apart from his leaf-green mantle and slippers, he was clothed from head to toe in shimmering gold, and on his head he wore a crown of bright yellow flower stamens.

"Kingcup!" breathed Zinnia, trembling a little as she curtseyed.

When she looked up, she saw that the king was smiling at her tenderly, and although this was the first time she had met him, she felt instantly at ease. As for the elves, they were a pathetic sight, cowering before the regal Flower Fairy, unrecognizable as the two creatures that had been taunting Zinnia just moments before.

"You are trespassing on Flower Fairy territory." Kingcup turned to them. "And for stealing from one of my kind, you are banished from the marsh—now be gone!"

The elves scrambled to their feet. "Yes, Your Majesty, many apologies, Your Majesty," they mumbled as they fell over each other to escape from the clearing first.

When they had gone, the king turned back to Zinnia with a twinkle in his eye. "Well, I think they were suitably told off, don't you? They don't really mean any harm; they just can't resist fairy cheese." He chuckled and then added, "or teasing!"

Zinnia breathed a sigh of relief. "Thank you so much for rescuing me," she said gratefully. "I realized fairly soon that they weren't dangerous—but they were maddening, and they wouldn't let me go."

"Presumably you mean home?" Kingcup said, taking Zinnia by the hand and leading her out of the clearing. Soon they had found the path, and as they walked he asked her, "What are you doing so far from the garden so late in the day?"

Zinnia began relaying the events of the afternoon, feeling a little foolish when it came to the part about showing off to the Wild Flower Fairies, but the king just smiled as if it was a mistake he could have easily made himself.

"Well," said Kingcup when she had finished, "I'm assuming that you'd like to go back to the garden tonight?" He waited for Zinnia to nod in response. "Then you're in luck. A dear friend of mine that is visiting will be heading back your way, and I'm sure she'd be more than glad to take you."

They'd left the path now and were picking their way across much wetter ground. Soon there were small pools of water, and it was not long before it was obvious to Zinnia that they had reached Kingcup's realm. Growing out of the pools were clusters of marsh marigolds with their kidney-shaped leaves and shiny golden flowers like giant buttercups. And sitting amongst them was a Flower Fairy with long blonde hair, delicate shell-pink wings, and a tiara of rose stamens.

"Wild Rose!" Zinnia cried out happily.

"So, I see your stroll was rather eventful," Wild Rose remarked to Kingcup as she fluttered over to join them. She kissed the top of Zinnia's head and murmured, "Sweet Garden Fairy, what are you doing here?"

"She's been having a grand adventure on the marsh," the king replied in good humor. "And I'm sure she'll tell you all about it on your way home."

"Oh yes, of course." Wild Rose nodded wisely. Then, glancing at the weary Garden Fairy, she said, "I think we'll summon a moorhen and see if we can catch a ride home."

Zinnia was very pleased to hear that they wouldn't be making the journey on foot, as ever since she had been in the comforting presence of Wild Rose, waves of tiredness had begun to wash over her. She would have gladly slept in precisely the spot she was standing. Once Kingcup had clapped his hands, they didn't have to wait for more than a few moments before a friendly looking bird with black glossy feathers and a vivid red-and-yellow beak landed in the water beside them. Without

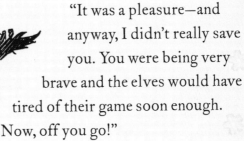

further ado, the king bade them farewell. "Good-bye, Rose, see you soon," he said, kissing her on both cheeks.

Zinnia watched Wild Rose mount the moorhen and sit elegantly with her legs and skirt to one side. Then she clambered up in front of her and wrapped her arms around the bird's neck in preparation for take-off.

"It was an honor to meet you, Your Majesty," she called to Kingcup. "Sorry you had to come and save me."

"It was a pleasure—and anyway, I didn't really save you. You were being very brave and the elves would have tired of their game soon enough. Now, off you go!"

* * *

185

"You know, I do enjoy living in the hedgerow and meeting all the Flower Fairies that pass by or come to visit me to be named. And I quite understand the lure of the unknown," said Wild Rose gently, "but you're very lucky to have a flower that resides out of harm's way. You always have a wonderful variety of company—so many different fairies to play with but all with familiar faces—as well as your own special butterfly friends."

Zinnia turned to say something in reply, but Wild Rose just raised a finger to her lips. "Look—here's the lane. We'll be there soon."

As they'd soared above the marsh, Zinnia had gazed down at the vast exposed area below, and she'd had a sense of just how small she was in comparison. Even with Wild Rose's arms encircling her waist, she'd suddenly felt quite lost, and as she listened to the words of the older Flower Fairy, she longed to be back in the garden. And there, far below them, but now in sight, was the garden. Zinnia's heart leaped at the sight of it and, with every ounce of her being, she willed the moorhen to fly faster.

186

Chapter Six
Bedtime Stories

"I didn't meet the Queen of the Meadow, but I did meet Kingcup!"
Zinnia was sitting on the edge of the moss blanket, under which Daisy
and Double Daisy were snuggled, telling her two little cousins all about her
adventure.

There had been great excitement when she had arrived on the back of the
moorhen. It wasn't often that Wild Rose visited the garden, but she had a
reputation as being the kindest and wisest of the Flower Fairies and was

greatly loved by all who knew her. Zinnia had proudly introduced Wild Rose to Daisy and Double Daisy—who lost no time in informing her all about their royal tea party and showing her their very best curtsy and bow, which Apple Blossom had been helping them perfect.

"Can you stay until bedtime?" Double Daisy had begged, after insisting that she come and see the corner of the garden that he and Daisy lived in, where their starlike flowers were still lifting their faces to catch the last rays of sunshine.

"I've had a very long day out on the moor," replied Wild Rose, "and it's time I was getting home, but I promise to come back for one of your splendid tea parties. Besides, I have a feeling that someone has a particularly interesting bedtime story to tell you tonight," she added, looking directly at Zinnia.

When they had said their good-byes and the Daisies had stopped jumping around at the thought of entertaining Wild Rose, Zinnia finally managed to settle them down for the night. The two little Flower Fairies sat upright in their bed, their blanket pulled up to their chins, and listened with shining eyes as she told them all about following the children to the marsh and how she had met Cotton-Grass, Rush-Grass, and Mallow.

They asked her to repeat the bit about the elves three times before she could get to the part where Kingcup rescued her and took her to find Wild Rose.

"What was the best part of the day?" Daisy asked, rubbing her eyes sleepily.

"Coming home to you two," Zinnia said without hesitation, leaning over to kiss them both good-night.

As the sun sank behind the garden wall and the last of the daisies closed its petals for the night, Zinnia sighed happily to herself. How could she ever get bored of the sight of her cousins sinking peacefully into sleep? She stood up and yawned. She couldn't imagine wanting to go off on an adventure for quite some time now, but the next time she did, it would be with the knowledge that the only place that she belonged at the end of the day was safely tucked up in her cozy corner of the garden.

POPPY FAIRY'S SONG

The green wheat's a-growing,
   The lark sings on high;
In scarlet silk a-glowing,
   Here stand I.

The wheat's turning yellow,
   Ripening for sheaves;
I hear the little fellow
   Who scares the bird-thieves.

Now the harvest's ended,
   The wheat-field is bare;
But still, red and splendid,
   I am there.

How To Be A Flower Fairy

WOULDN'T IT BE WONDERFUL to be a real Flower Fairy, living among the flowers and trees with all your fairy friends? If you love this idea, there are lots of ways you can be just like a Flower Fairy. Start off by reciting this enchanted rhyme:

"I close my eyes and count to five
To make the fairies come alive.
And when I open them, I see
There is a brand-new fairy—me!"

Flower Fairies love nature and know all about plants and animals.
If you have a garden, explore it in every season or just
keep your eyes open when you're outside or in the park.
You never know what you'll find!

You could make a nature collection of the things you discover, such
as pinecones, pebbles, flowers, and leaves. Why not decorate a shoe box
with pretty paper and ribbon to make a special place for your collection?

Like the fairies, always try to be kind and helpful and take care of the
animals and plants around you.

The Fairy Code

If you want to be like a fairy, you must know
the Fairy Code. Even the naughtiest fairies try
to keep to these rules!
Always try to be:
❀ Cheerful
❀ Neat
❀ Polite
❀ Friendly
❀ Hardworking
❀ Honest
❀ Good at keeping secrets
❀ Kind

YOUR FAIRY NAME

Follow the arrows through the trail of leaves below.
Pick the words you like the most, and they'll lead
you to your first fairy name, in the green leaf.
Do this again on the next page to discover
your second fairy name!

START HERE!

PINK
BLUE

SPRING
SUMMER
AUTUMN
WINTER

ICE CREAM
JELLY
APPLE
PEAR
NUTS
BERRIES
CHOCOLATE
CAKE

STRAWBERRY
ROSE
APPLE BLOSSOM
PEAR BLOSSOM
ACORN
BLACKBERRY
HOLLY
SNOWDROP

My name is Snowdrop Ice-Web!

Use the below trail to work out the second part of your fairy name.

I'm Pear Blossom Elf-Glitter!

BUTTERFLIES

TWINKLE

MEADOW

LADYBIRDS

SWEET-SHIMMER

SUN

BEACH

HIDING

ELF-GLITTER

SEEKING

SILVER-WAND

START HERE!

FOREST

POEMS

STARLIGHT

STARS

STORIES

MOONSHINE

LAKE

FEATHERFOOT

DANCING

ICE-WEB

SINGING

You will need:

Newspaper

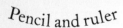

Pencil and ruler

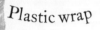

Scissors

Plastic wrap

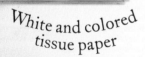

White and colored tissue paper

Craft glue

Cardboard

Paintbrush

Elastic cord

Hole punch

HELIOTROPE'S FAIRY WINGS

Here's how to make your very own pair of beautiful, shimmering Flower Fairy wings.

1. Fold a sheet of newspaper in half and draw the shape of the upper and lower wings on it. These are your templates. Draw half the wings only, starting from the center-fold.

2. Keeping the paper folded, cut out the two templates. Unfold the wings and cover them with a large sheet of plastic wrap.

3. Lay a sheet of white tissue paper over the wings and paint with a solution of two parts glue to one part water. Add four more sheets in the same way.

4. Glue on four smaller sheets of purple tissue paper in the same way, as shown. Let them dry, then peel off the plastic wrap.

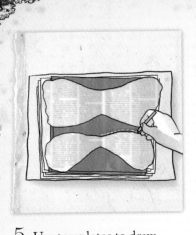

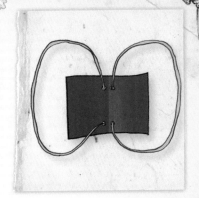

5. Use templates to draw around and cut out your wings. Stick smaller wings on to larger wings, about half way down (see main picture).

6. Cut out a rectangular piece of cardboard, about 5 inches x 4 inches. Now make four holes in the card using a hole punch.

7. Cut out two pieces of elastic, each about 16 inches long. Thread each piece through the holes in the cardboard and tie in a knot at the back.

Decorate your wings with glued-on sequins and a sprinkle of glitter.

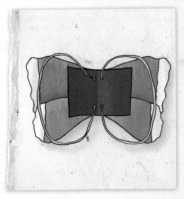

8. Glue the card to the back of the wings. Now put your arms through the elastic and flutter like a Flower Fairy!

Magic Fairy Spells

Spells are an important part of the Flower Fairies' world. And although there are a mixture of naughty and nice fairies, they always use their magic powers to do good.

The Sunshine Spell

To bring out the sun, make a chain of buttercups and wear them in your hair. Spin around three times and repeat this rhyme . . .

'Glitter, glimmer magic sun, shine your light on everyone!'

THE BIRTHDAY SPELL

When it's your birthday, make a wish while planting seeds. Your wish should grow with your plant!

'Pretty plant, I do love you, please grow and make my wish come true!'

THE RAIN SPELL

Take a cup of water and add a few blades of grass. Using a twig, stir three times to the left and three times to the right, then pour the potion on to the roots of the tree. It should soon rain!

'Pitter, patter, drops of rain, feed the garden once again!'

Good Night, Flower Fairies!

Every Flower Fairy needs a good night's sleep to be at her very best! To sleep like a fairy, why not try these two flower remedies? Remember, always ask an adult before picking any flowers.

Scented Bathing

Sometimes there's nothing better than a bath before bed to send you right off to sleep!

❀ Get permission to pick some flowers and leave them to dry for a few days in a warm place.

❀ Carefully pluck the petals from the flowers.

❀ Ask an adult to help you run a nice warm bath, and add a little bath oil. Scatter the petals over the surface of the bath, and enjoy!

LOVELY LAVENDER

❀ Cut a bunch of flowering lavender and put it in a vase without water. It will smell delicious and should take just a few days to dry out naturally.

❀ Remove the lavender stalks, and put a handful of lavender in the middle of a handkerchief.

❀ Gather the sides together and tie with a pretty ribbon. Then store it with your bed linen or put under your pillow.

❀ The soothing scent of lavender will soon help you drift off to sleep!

SLEEP TIGHT!

"Say good-bye to this precious day,
It's been full of magic, fun, and play!
It's time for the fairies to bid you good night,
Have sweet dreams; we hope you sleep tight!"

Fairy Farewell

Now that you have come to the end of the book, you know everything there is to know about the Flower Fairies. You have learned about the different kinds of fairies and the secret world in which they live, work, and play. And if you are trying to find a fairy, you will know exactly what to look for. But remember—fairies don't like to be discovered, and they are very shy and secretive around humans. They are also good at disappearing quickly, so you will have to be very patient and careful if you are to see one.

Remember that fairies only ever reveal themselves to those who believe in them. And if you are ever lucky enough to spot one, it is important to keep it secret—if too many people find out about the Flower Fairies, their world could be in danger.

It is thought that the best times of the day to see a fairy are at twilight, midnight, just before sunrise, and midday. The best time of the year to see a fairy is in June, on Midsummer's Eve, as this is the most magical time for all fairies. So be on the lookout for tiny, colorful wings and listen for the tinkling sound of fairy singing and laughter!

Tread gently now, there may be a Flower Fairy afoot....

GLOSSARY

Acorn Fairy

Alder Fairy

Almond Blossom Fairy

Apple Blossom Fairies

Ash Tree Fairy

Beech Tree Fairy

Beechnut Fairy

Bird's-Foot Trefoil Fairy

Blackberry Fairy

Black Bryony Fairy

Black Medick Fairies

Bluebell Fairy

Bugle Fairy

Burdock Fairy

Buttercup Fairy

Candytuft Fairy

Canterbury Bell Fairy

Cherry Tree Fairy

Chicory Fairy

Christmas Tree Fairy

Columbine Fairies

Cornflower Fairy

Crab-Apple Fairy

Crocus Fairies

GLOSSARY

Daffodil Fairy

Daisy Fairy

Dogwood Fairy

Double Daisy Fairy

Elder Fairy

Elderberry Fairy

Elm Tree Fairy

Forget-me-not Fairies

Fuchsia Fairy

Fumitory Fairy

Gaillardia Fairy

Geranium Fairy

Gorse Fairies

Grape Hyacinth Fairy

Greater Celandine Fairy

Ground Ivy Fairy

Guelder Rose Fairies

Harebell Fairy

Hawthorn Fairy

Hazel-Nut Fairy

Heather Fairy

Heliotrope Fairy

Herb Robert Fairy

Herb Twopence Fairy

GLOSSARY

Holly Fairy

Honeysuckle Fairy

Horse Chestnut Fairy

Iris Fairy

Jack-go-to-bed-at-noon Fairy

Jasmine Fairy

Kingcup Fairy

Laburnum Fairy

Lavender Fairy

Lilac Fairy

Lime Tree Fairy

Lords-and-Ladies Fairy

Mallow Fairy

Marigold Fairy

Michaelmas Daisy Fairy

Mountain Ash Fairy

Mulberry Fairy

Narcissus Fairy

Nasturtium Fairy

Nightshade Berry Fairy

Old-Man's-Beard Fairy

Pansy Fairy

Pear Blossom Fairy

Periwinkle Fairy

GLOSSARY

Phlox Fairy

Pine Tree Fairy

Pink Fairies

Poplar Fairy

Poppy Fairy

Primrose Fairy

Privet Fairy

Queen of the
Meadow Fairy

Ragged Robin
Fairy

Red Campion
Fairy

Red Clover Fairy

Ribwort Plantain
Fairy

Robin's
Pincushion Fairy

Rose Fairy

Rose Hip Fairy

Rose-Bay Willow-
Herb Fairy

Rush-Grass and
Cotton-Grass Fairies

Scabious Fairy

Scilla Fairy

Self-Heal Fairy

Shirley Poppy
Fairy

Sloe Fairy

Silver Birch Fairy

Snapdragon Fairy

GLOSSARY

 Snowdrop Fairy

 Speedwell Fairy

 Sweet Chestnut Fairy

 Sweet Pea Fairies

 Stork's-bill Fairy

 Strawberry Fairy

 Sycamore Fairy

 Tansy Fairy

 Totter-grass Fairy

 Tulip Fairy

 Vetch Fairy

 Wallflower Fairy

 Wayfaring Tree Fairy

 White Bindweed Fairy

 White Bryony Fairy

 Wild Cherry Blossom Fairy

 Wild Thyme Fairy

 Willow Fairy

 Winter Aconite Fairy

 Winter Jasmine Fairy

 Wood-Sorrel Fairy

 Yellow Deadnettle Fairy

 Yew Fairy

 Zinnia Fairy